The Epic of Clair

An Epic Poem

E.C. Hansen

ILIUM
PRESS

Spokane Valley, Washington, USA
www.iliumpress.com

The Epic of Clair: An Epic Poem

Copyright © 2014 by Eric C. Hansen. All rights reserved.

This book has been composed in Constantia.

Cover design: Kenyon Sharp
Book design: John Lemon

The Epic of Clair / an epic poem [by] Eric C. Hansen.
ISBN 978-0-9833002-6-7 (pbk.)
ISBN 978-0-9833002-7-4 (ePub)

Library of Congress Control Number: 2014942416
Library of Congress subject headings:
1. Epic poetry, English
I. Hansen, Eric Charles, 1974 – . II. Title

Published and printed in the United States of America by the Ilium Press,
Spokane Valley, Washington, U.S.A.

All books from the Ilium Press are printed on high quality, acid-free,
book-grade opaque paper stock that meets ANSI standards for archival
quality paper. Binding materials are chosen for strength and durability.

Visit the Ilium Press online at www.iliumpress.com.

For Alison

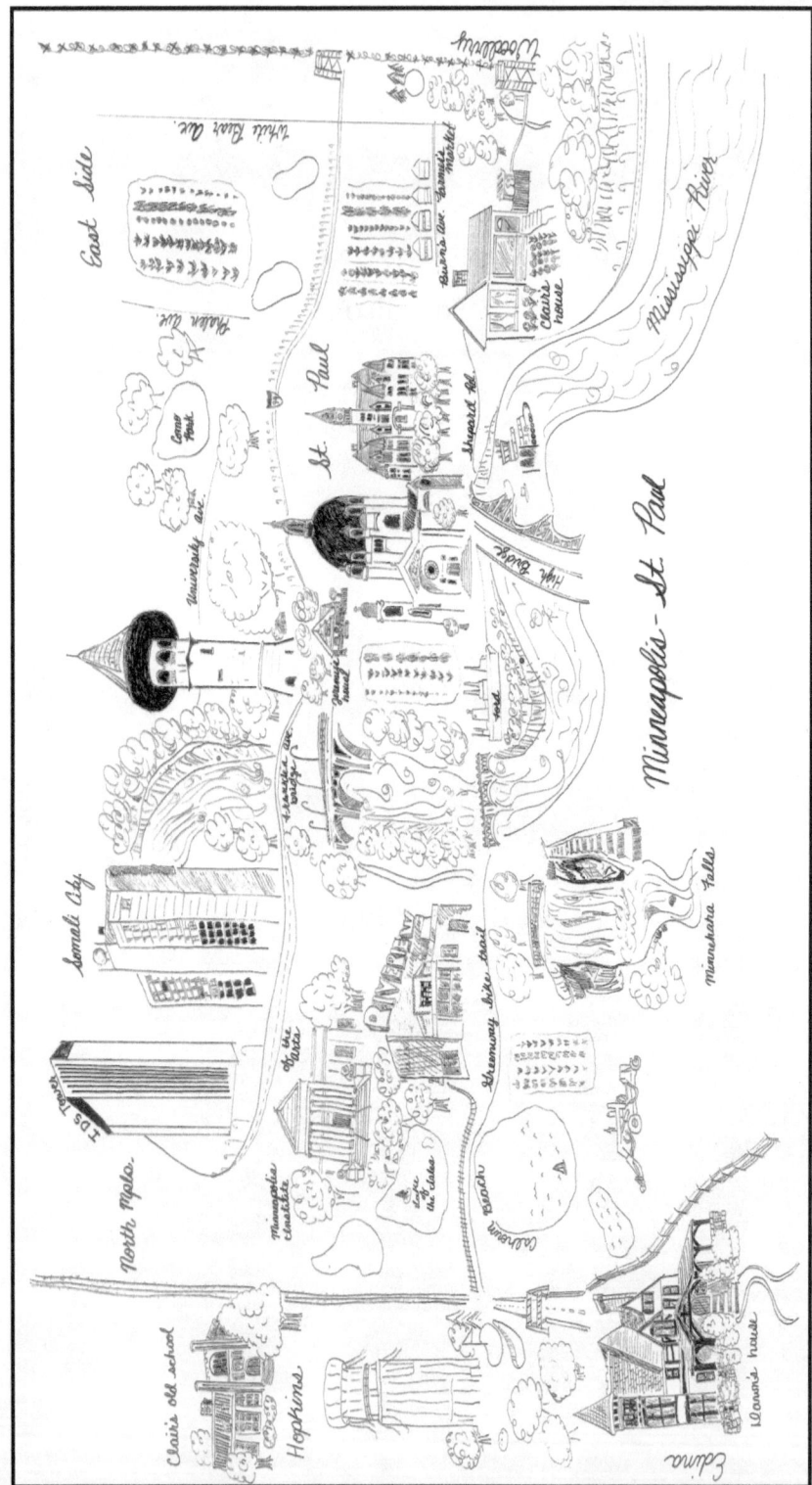

Contents

CONTENTS

Dramatis Personae

Character	Age	Description
Clair Ibsen	15	Bright but seriously anxious former cross-country star and school writing prize winner. No longer attending school. Lives in working-class East St. Paul, Minnesota.
Paul Ibsen	45	Father of Clair and husband to Mary. Former private-school English teacher. Now unemployed, he writes metered, unpublished poems in his study.
Mary Ibsen	43	Mother of Clair and wife to Paul. Minnesota-certified master gardener. Grows vegetables to barter at Burns Avenue Farmer's Market.
Dawn Arbaugh	15	Friend and former classmate to Clair. Boy crazy but shy. Lives in wealthy Edina, Minnesota.
Victoria Arbaugh	52	Mother of Dawn and wife to Derek Arbaugh. Studied painting at Carleton College, later licensed as an interior decorator but never practiced.
Derek Arbaugh	48	Father of Dawn and husband to Victoria. Chief executive at a major international bank. BA, MBA, and JD from Yale. Gave $3 million to charity in 2007.
Nat Mortensen	16	Former schoolmate to Clair. Expelled in his sophomore year. Heir to Kohl family gas refining and retail fortune. Three-time school spelling bee champion. Parents divorced.

Character	Age	Description
Jeremy	54	Born in Newcastle, England. Classically trained pianist and violinist, later singer and keyboard player of a punk band. Also composed symphonies for orchestras in Beirut and Budapest. Now father of twins. Lives in Prospect Park neighborhood of Minneapolis.
Alessandra	6	Jeremy's daughter.
Cassandra	6	Jeremy's daughter.
Hermes	Immortal	Greek messenger god, as well as trickster, god of commerce, lord of thieves, and guide of souls.
Jessica Conrad	41	Elegant witch.
Mrs. Smith	78	Witch leader.
Mrs. Jones	62	Copy editor to witches.
Anna	17	Chatty witch. Works in the tower print shop.
Milocz Kocinski	29	Polish operator of Vulcan Open Source Engineering. PhD from Warsaw University of Technology.
Troy	16	Vampire boy.
Troy's women	15–16	Assorted vampire girlfriends.
Dying man	83	
Touger Lor	37	Former performance artist. Leader of Eastside Hmong Clans.
Y'Vonne Johnson	29	Chief physician of North Minneapolis health clinic for women and children. Medical degree from University of Minnesota.
John Stilgoe	Unknown (records unavailable)	Former Minneapolis city council member. Presently homeless spokesperson for Tent People.

A Note About Form

A book's form should fit its themes. For reasons you are soon to see, *The Epic of Clair* is told in the most ancient of literary forms.

A proper epic bears certain marks:

1. The story begins with an invocation to the muses;
2. A descent into the underworld and divine intervention are entirely possible;
3. An epic demands its hero—in this case, a girl with fleet feet.

Suitably then, most of this book's lines race along in blank verse, or unrhymed iambic pentameter, the poetic meter favored by Shakespeare. (A few characters do speak with different meters, especially in Chapter 22.)

Basically, meter governs the rhythm of a poetic line. Two neighboring syllables sound harsher, longer, or stronger *in relation to each other*. Thus, a single iamb sounds like a down-beat followed by an UP-beat. The term pentameter merely refers to five such iambic pairings:

Two HOUSE|holds BOTH | aLIKE | in DIG|niTY

Many fine resources available online explain poetic meter in greater detail. Perhaps the clearest, most helpful book on the subject is Alfred Corn's *The Poem's Heartbeat: A Manual of Prosody*.

However, understanding poetic form is *not* necessary to enjoy *The Epic of Clair*. The poet took pains to avoid a dusty tone.

Just know, O reader, nothing is accidental. *Run with it.*

We are lived by powers we pretend to understand:
They arrange our loves; it is they who direct at the end
The enemy bullet, the sickness, or even our hand.
— W.H. Auden

Chapter 1

Vertigo and the Importance of Ten

Heavens, help me tell the story about
that girl-runner who saved her parents' house
and beat her own anxiety problems
by running messages for the witches
after the oil economy's collapse.
Time reversed itself in 2008.
Hence, I am calling upon the old bards,
their method of telling heroic tales
in lines of poetry that run place to
place like the girl we will call Clair Ibsen.   10
She paced herself around ten miles per hour;
no wonder then the spirit who whispered
her tale to me preferred pentameter.

Let me start with the causes of Clair's grief.
Imagine in '08 all the deep-sea
oil rigs and global derricks drew zilch but
mud, water, and groans. Reserves could be tapped,
but soon prices grew in asymptotic
slopes.

Clair's father the poet couldn't drive
himself and her across the metro to   20
the great prep school where he taught and she aced
ninth grade. The cheap ride was over. Highways
opened up to bicycles in one lane,
two lanes for the rich in electric cars
and the super-rich in black SUVs.

Clair's tuition was free, and her father
was much admired, but he couldn't afford
the commute now. Gas was finer than gold.
The school mourned the loss of both, but twenty
miles lay between Edina and where they   30
lived in a bungalow in East St. Paul.

Bad news next came in a snail-mail letter.
Only the corporations could manage
to send a mailman anymore. Other-
wise people sent a text. Neighbors looked up
when a carrier came. Clair's dad had been
in his study, the extra bedroom, where
he now made homeschool lessons for Clair and
wrote long, irregular, metered poems
on pages from discarded phone books. He   40
heard the mail Jeep—the only motor sound
outside of the highways—and paused his pen.
His wife, Clair's mother, could be heard talking
to the stranger. They had feared what they knew
had come then, what did not come to neighbors
who owned their homes which they'd bought long before.

But Clair's parents got their mortgage later
in '04 for an optimistic price.

They told Clair the sad news after dinner:
they had no way to pay the bank's monthly   50
bill. Their house was entering foreclosure.

"I thought I had it hard when I lost school,"
Clair said. "Now I see how hard hard can be."
Her parents insisted things would work out.
But Clair pictured the loss of the garden,
the hydrangea, peonies, coneflowers
she'd set into the ground with her mother,
the pergola her dad had built for her
to rest in shade and read on summer days,
the scalloped cedar fence inside which she   60
felt like a Persian princess. Paradise,
soon to be lost: the room where she'd played dolls—
an eternity ago but mere years;
oak planks of the living room floor made blonde
in the trapezoid shape of late sunlight;
the cool slate kitchen tiles her father set
and argued over with Mom at Christmas.
They had made this house their sanctuary.
And the oil collapse made the neighborhood
more than a 'hood. Clair got up from dinner—   70
always the light eater—and went to bed.

She heard the study door click quietly,
her father already returning to
his endless lines of odd, unpublished verse,

the clink of dishes, her mom cleaning up.
Ever fraught with the ailment of the age,
anxiety, Clair—who freaked out on tests
and felt sick before cross-country races—
lost her balance now. The world orbited
her bed. The red spelling-bee ribbon spun.   80
She cried for her parents like a mere child.
They rushed in, saw her huge-eyed, unable
to turn her head a centimeter left
or right, frozen, a panicked opossum.

"Sit up," her mom said, "and stare at some fixed
spot on the wall." She pulled, but Clair groaned hard.

"Should we call an ambulance?" her dad asked.

Clair protested (her head still planted straight
on the throw pillows). *Another bad debt!*
The cost would be terrible! Lots of folks   90
suffered in the world, billions to be true,
but nobody knew misery more than
this vertigo. Clair, the most pathetic
girl on the planet, only wanted this
to end, and the more she willed an ending,
the harder she spun. And worse, her bladder
was full from dinner. She needed to pee!
She sat up but—*No!* Back down she collapsed.
If God existed, then He was evil.
The misery that's possible in life!   100
How blithely people walk without a thought.
Clair hugged the walls. A family photo crashed.

She tried to outstep the seeming tempest—
like a sailor who knows the ship will heave
one way—and fell before the toilet bowl.
Vomit and urine mixed together there.
(They tended to let the yellow mellow.)
Again, the shanty dance back to her bed.
There she lay, spent and tossed, wishing for death.

Chapter 2

Janice Chang and the Three Horsemen

Clair's mother gave her some sleeping capsules.
She might as well have been buried out back
where bulbs and nuts rest inert all winter,
black, dreamless, but not exactly lifeless.
One-hundred-percent life in potential.
The sun rose next day. Her eyelids lifted.
Her father sat close by her side with his
copy of *Purgatorio* held close.
This was Clair's bedroom, Clair's house—but not hers,
not *her* house, nor *her* room. She remembered   10
the bank's claim upon her family's future.
Her mother's drugs were weaker than memory.

The world tilted. *Whoa!*—here she went again.
She tried to scramble free from vertigo.
The world resumed its whirling—terrible.
Over her father's legs, out the doorway,
a wrestling match against the hallway walls,
more portraits fell, refusing Mother's pleas,
she shuttle-ran across the living room—
damn how the deadbolt sticks! Clair abandoned   20

the house. She anteloped past pink coneflowers
in the front yard, forgetting about shoes.
It made no sense, but she ran while dizzy.
The sky was bathwater, blue-white and warm.
Clair took to the carless road, wide enough
for a drunkard's weave. Yet she straightened out.
Her strides were short, rapid, tapping her soles.
Gardeners in their boulevard beds observed
her race against Grief, Despair, Vertigo—
the three horsemen of her apocalypse   30
in a swift pack, chewing road behind her.

Last fall's cross-country state championships
bore a resemblance to the current race:
the team from East Wayzata dogged her tail,
hounds behind the fox, but they shielded in
their rapid pace a leader, Janet Chang,
who coasted behind her friends' snow-plow push.
In the last mile, behind the bend of pines,
Clair heard a catbird-like chirp—a tricky
move!—and gawked back to see if someone fell.   40
The pack charged its last and caught up to Clair.
With officials yet out of sight, they crammed
Clair's strides—no pushes, nothing that vicious.
Janet sprung the cage, the trail straightened toward
the end, and everyone cheered the girl's spring.

Just so, the horsemen of nervous breakdowns
threatened to cut short Clair's barefoot progress.
What did second place mean in such a race?
She couldn't hazard it. But run how long?

Her feet felt fleet without her running shoes.   50
Workmen's bungalows followed each other,
identical but for the stucco paint.
Boys playing football games dodged around her.
Cars did not sit tireless in the roadway
like in post-nuclear-war movies. The road,
Burns Avenue, became on most weekends
an extended farmer's (or flea) market.
Neighbors spent these early June days outside;
few had employment to leave their homes for.
Thus, nobody could pay for power and   60
spend the whole day inside, watching TV.
The garden women, the bike-cart haulers,
men chopping trees down, self-deputized toughs,
teenage girls strutting the catwalk all day,
a grandma chasing a bantam rooster,
urban rednecks erecting wind turbines,
men on storm drains who preached from their black books,
Hmong teens intoning gibes between maize rows
and the sides of front-yard volleyball courts,
Latin men putting up walls of limestone,   70
black families buying and selling their goods
from sidewalks—none of them had any rush,
except for Clair, a winged figure, free.

The secret of her speed: her small body
her undeveloped frame, her narrow hips
barely hoisted a hundred pounds, lighter
than she was strong, and her lungs knew no pain.

Clair slowed at the city line where fences
protected suburban cars, gas, and fear.

Grown men with varsity jackets and guns   80
watched from scaffolding towers. They cried out
at the running girl, "Hey! Did you get lost?
Is your home over here, in Woodbury?"

Clair, confused, said no. An empty Coke can
was thrown at her, but lamely fell well short.
"Get back to your ghetto, then," one man sneered.
"I'll try to find you a pair of Nikes!"

Her return run began. She realized
then, in spite of the buffoons, how splendid
her flight felt now. Her fear was exhausted.   90
Clair had triumphed over her nervousness.

When she reached home, she brushed off her parents,
"I'm fine, Mom and Dad. I went for a run."
And poured herself a bath. Her feet were on fire.

Chapter 3

Spinning in High Gear

The peas were almost ready to pluck. Then
they'd keep for weeks in the cool, dark basement.
Lettuces in June regrew right after
one took the leaves. Broccoli grew since March.

The old 24-hour supermarket
had closed. Food came in its own good season.
The backyard had been squared into raised beds
with Clair's father's third-rate carpentry and
her mom's green thumb, which never made money
before the collapse but now traded well.   10
Clair crouched, picking weeds, knowing they desired
to rise and breathe as well as the sweet peas
strung high on the frame. Still, she yanked them out,
a firm finger grasp close to the surface.
The better to pull out a weed for good.
Her calves ached from her barefoot escapade.
She played the toad, weeding without rising.
But no vertigo! She'd exhausted herself.
What if she thought about...no, not so soon.

A day outside still could be beautiful.   20
Pods of clouds did not care about "home."
And no longer were they herded by planes
or fenced in by contrails. The sky was clear.

How many varieties of flower,
vegetable, insect, and amphibian
occupied the garden? Not even Mom
knew, though she'd been the one who brought them here,
usually half-dead from the side of the road
or sun-baked from an end-of-summer sale.
Given the right conditions, the near-dead lived.   30

Clair pondered this while above sat the jade
plant on the patio table, huge, god-
like in its big blue pot, which started as
a twig and one cankered, unshining leaf.
The jade plant wintered in the living room,
but in June, Clair and her dad brought it out
to overlook its fellow greens.

                         But where
were Clair's fellows, her friends? Swimming in pools
the size of the house she was soon to lose?
Living high on the hog near school in wealth?   40
In the halls, between classes, she used to
overlook their privilege. Dawn, Gabi, Rain,
and the rest, came from money—doctors, big
bankers, CEOs of Target. Tycoons.
Still, she wished she could be with her old pals,

wherever they were lazing. But she couldn't.
Her family still kept a Ford Taurus
in the garage with an empty gas tank.
Perhaps Clair'd be one of those eccentrics
who never left home like old Dickinson,   50
the spinster poet who loved God and bees.
Now cutting broccoli—tiny green brains—
Clair was a girl of many minds.

                    What if
she packed a lunch and rode her bike to Dawn?
Edina lay a marathon away but
nothing that a ten-speed couldn't traverse.
She'd ridden with Dad on Bike-to-School Day.

Another weed yanked. She waited to ask,
not for fear of "No," but to hold the taste
of a journey, of freedom, in her mouth.   60

Then, at dinner, the meal dedicated
to dream-dashing talk, she posed her wild plan.

"Sure," her mom said, "if you crank up my cell phone
and call Dad's phone when you get there and leave."
(They owned a hand-cranked battery charger.)

Dad sat, silent. Then nodded. Clair fueled up
on sweet peas, broccoli, and romaine hearts.
After dinner, she called Dawn's house and asked.
Her friend talked to *her* mom, came back, and: "Yes!"

Next day, Clair packed her lunch with leftovers.   70
Never before had her lunchbox felt keen
and happy like it did in her backpack
now. At school she always felt like a dweeb
pulling cheese sandwiches from her lunchbox
while others could afford to eat a feast,
private school food, chefs manning sides of beef,
slicing the choicest cuts, all you could eat.
A teacher's benefits couldn't pay that expense
in a time of skyrocketing food costs.
Now lunch felt special, a traveler's fare,   80
like leaf-wrapped elf bread in *Lord of the Rings*.
Her mother went through a pre-trip checklist.
Lunch box? *Check.*

           Cell phone charged? *Check.*

                      Water? *Check.*

Bike tuned up? Chain greased? *Check.*

                  Folding knife? *Check.*

The knife—Dad's contribution to the trip.
He'd never used it, but it was his dad's,
Grandpa Leigh's fishing knife. Cruel-looking blade,
too, long and curved when unhinged. Bone-handled,
yet made to debone. Clair carried it closed
in a fanny pack that made her feel old,   90
fat, and German, but that at least stayed out
of her way.

      "Dear, call us when you get there,"
Mom practically sang. *Was she sad or not?*

Clair's bike began with a roll down the hill
to the river's edge where she pedaled fast
on Shepard Road, skipping the sidewalk where
kids hawked produce from tables a few feet
near where parents tilled guerilla gardens
in the river park. Everyone traded.
Serenity described the afternoon   100
sky. High wisps, infant ribs, the only clouds.
Clair played with gears, never settling on one,
so the bike clacked a lot. Finally she
selected fifth or sixth, she couldn't tell,
an okay middle between push and spin.
She admired the defunct tugboats moored
along the great river's edge, suggestive
of ocean ports, not the Mississippi.
She did not look up under the High Bridge,
its lofty span aimed at the cathedral,   110
from which many men jumped when their jobs stopped,
the river acting as undertaker.
Clair spun her feet in circles, and she soon
passed the big, empty Ford plant and the bridge
which she crossed hogging the solid gold line
into Minneapolis.

                    An eagle
perched sentry nearby, nest big as a fridge.
Clair now followed the Nokomis Creek trail;
the path was busier than any road—
bicycles, carts, pedestrians, a horse—   120
they moved at a speed where one saw faces,

14

sometimes downcast or seeking others' eyes—
a giant royal puppet retinue
(courtiers with tip jars and black tights)—
old ladies with turnips in shopping carts—
the fellow selling cell phones—teenagers
on tiny BMX bikes—the homeless
who did not blink in search of some safe spot.

Near a kiddy pool, Clair stopped and ate lunch,
then she headed west on Fiftieth Ave.   130
It used to be, the line between city
and first-ring suburb was vague, indistinct.
One-story ramblers and chain coffee shops.
Now a posse manned a closed gate checkpoint,
men with duck boots, L.L. Bean cargo pants,
polos with logos, oily black rifles.
Clair pulled up on France Street, her brakes squeaking.

"Where are you riding to by yourself, girl?"
a guard with a yoga-toned body said.

Clair, the sweet girl, not a liar, per se,   140
knew why she'd won the eighth-grade writing prize—
through the trick of excessive detail. No
other could match her verisimilitude.
She recalled the art of storytelling:

"My parents are divorced, Mom took it all—
the house on Lake Minnetonka, Charlie
and Tom, our well-bred golden-doodle pups,
the hybrid Range Rover, Dad's collection

of hand-carved duck decoys. He's left with zip
in his small, greasy apartment over   150
Matt's Jucy Lucy, the best burger joint
around"—the men nodded their heads—"and I
chose to live with him in penury out
of love for my jobless, forlorn father.
But he sends me now to my mom across
the sad split between our communities
to plea one more time for medical help.
His testicular cancer is awful—"

The men looked away, up at the sky, now
clouded in octopus ink. They cursed Fate   160
that could be this cruel. "Go," the leader said,
pulling the barrier ajar, "get help."

Clair pedaled past golf courses and lawns like
golf courses. In driveways: well-washed autos.
Toes down, heels up, she rode as if she ran.
So many times she had hung out at Dawn's
house, like a chateau, before meets, concerts,
or when her dad had after-school meetings.
Clair found it just as she remembered it.
Glad, she rode up the flagstone Candy-Land   170
driveway toward the rounded ginger-bread door.

Chapter 4

This Heaven

Dawn with her rosy red fingers opened
up and reached for a hug—such a good friend.
She was thin, fair, with big bewildered eyes
as though she couldn't find her eyeglasses.
In classes her voice had been trembly or
unheard at all, but Clair knew the real Dawn,
a girl who wrote wicked text messages
and online comments under the login
dontmesswiththisredhairednymph563.
The shiest girl in school was boy crazy.   *10*
Hence, Dawn was funny to be around but
also perennially frustrated.

Her mom came and greeted Clair graciously,
yet she looked like a thin librarian,
one who insisted on total silence.
Dawn's dad, a banker, was never in town.

They went up to the bedroom with a bag
of red, spicy cheese curls—the best! Dawn said,
"Everybody was really bummed when you

were gone cause we figured we'd never see   20
you again. I tried texting you two times,
but a guy named Tim has your old number.
So I've struck up a bond with him instead!"
They laughed. Dawn had the prettiest white teeth.

Clair, the smallest, fastest girl in school, but
also the English teacher's kid, opened up.
"Well, to be honest, my life rots right now.
I can't see anyone we were friends with,
and my life is so different in my 'ghetto,'
plus—promise you won't tell anyone else—   30
but we're going to lose our little house!
When I found out, I got really dizzy.
Oh, God, I'm so nervous about the future."
Dawn gave the obligatory girl hug.
Behind her was a poster of some hunk.

They watched TV plugged into a socket,
no battery crank, no generator,
no modified diesel engine roaring
outside on vegetable oil and old lard.
The homes of rich friends felt like museums,
dustless places with clean white walls, winding   40
stairways, fine objects to see but don't touch,
at once so much more clear-headed than home.
Clair wanted to sit in the middle with
a cup of green tea and breathe luxury.
Then she'd go home and feel melancholic
for a week, unable to turn on lights,
only to wait for sleep with classical

music on her batteried radio
until she'd wake by chance to Debussy,
or her song, *Clair du Lune*—when her funk would quit.   50
At least that's how her past visits ended.

In Dawn's room, cognizant of the slow, cold
finger-touch of—O!—air-conditioning,
Clair recognized this comfort and giddy
glee as cousin to the alcoholic's
binge. Bring on TV's intoxication!
They watched a unit that still had cable.
The clatter of rain against the windows
just made the air cleaner, the screen clearer.

It was hard to know how long Dawn's mother   60
had stood in the corner like a docent
who minds a gallery, but when she spoke
to call the girls for supper, Clair woke up.
A man in a delivery truck
had brought a smorgasbord—French brie cheese,
rosemary crackers in a cellophane-
wrapped box, oranges from Florida and fresh
red grapes, not dried old raisins. The best, though,
was sushi, Clair's favorite, the cutest cuts
of avocado, cucumber, and sweet   70
potato—an inconceivable feast.
The expense for shipping these foods from far
away must have been huge in the oil crunch.

Dawn's mom said they could use the heated sun-
room pool. The girls had plenty of time left

before dark, though Clair forgot her own suit.
She borrowed a black one-piece race Speedo,
too long and tight. Yet the pool was better
by far than any creek or weedy lake
she might enter on the east side of town.   80
Again, the cleanness! Underwater, Clair
suspended herself inside this heaven's
blue-white, shadow-waving walls. The hot tub
almost put her to sleep, but Dawn announced
the news report on their mutual friends.

Gabi got kicked off the school newspaper
for penning a controversial piece.
Nat, the boy everybody used to think
was autistic, had been caught selling drugs,
prescription meds, pain relievers, and pills   90
meant to zero in on anxiety.
Clair gasped. This was the Nat who in eighth grade
threw a crying fit for late homework.

"And what about Rain?" she asked, "How is she?"

Dawn explained she never came to visit
anymore. She was obsessed with growing
flowers and food, "a wannabe pauper."

Clair was about to protest when Dawn left
saying she'd be right back. The hot tub boiled
away. Dawn returned with her mom and towels.   100

Without crouching near the edge of the tub,
Dawn's mother said, soothing, "Dawn told me where
you live—I can barely believe you came
all that way and through the urban jungle.
Now it's grown late, and we must invite,
or insist, you stay. Do your parents
still own a phone?"

             Clair accepted a towel.
Of course a sleepover made perfect sense.
"Yes, I'll call them," Clair said, rising from warmth.
She sent a text and within ten minutes   110
received an email: *Have a nice time, dear.*

They rode in a Land Rover into town—
"town" in this case being Edina, not
Minneapolis. With a TV on,
tinted windows, more air conditioning,
Clair knew this was the prom ride she'd never
get.

    In the chic cafe, how weird it was,
already, for someone to serve them sweets.
As if the feast before wasn't enough!
Dawn's mom had German double-chocolate cake.   120
Dawn picked at a kiwi-berry torte, and
Clair, who ordered turtle cheesecake, watched
the surrounding well-heeled families eat.
But none looked quite glad for the masterpiece
confectionaries. Their arms walled their plates.

21

Well, Clair saw each bite as a limited-
time offer, so she told herself, *Even
if I die a pathetic, early death
I will know I tasted this piece of cake!*
Nobody said much during her triumph.   130

The girls stayed up to watch 1980s
movies about teen delinquents in love.
They recorded their favorite lines with Dawn's
smart phone and played them back "on air," pranking
the Home Shopping Channel (Oil Edition).
Tired, delirious, they brushed their teeth.
Clair lay down in a day bed in Dawn's room.
Her friend, in a high bed against the wall,
formed a plateau of pillows. As people
in fancier times did, she slept sitting.   140
Lights out. The sky had cleared in time to see
the stars out a big bay window. Clair said,
"Dawn, I'm pooped. It's the sugar. No more sleep-
overs for me."

       Dawn's voice sounded back,
a magical echo in the darkness.
"But don't you see? It's like Harry Potter!
You're Harry, and we're your friends, the Weasleys.
We rescued you from that lame Privet Drive,
so you don't have to stay there the summer."

Clair laughed at the fantasy but then lay   150
without a word. This was a holiday,
but the truth hung in front of Clair, brightly,

like a neon sign outside the window.
Some people found life far, far easier
than others. And she wasn't as lucky.

They woke ridiculously late for Clair.
A front overnight had squeegeed the sky.
Dawn pointed up as if picking out clothes.

"It's such a dilemma: my dad wants me
to go to Yale, his *alma mater*, but   160
my mom wants me to go to Carleton."

She showed how she could make a damn fine mug
of coffee with a single-serve machine
she fed cartridges. Is this how college
might feel with its freedoms and depth charges?
What if Clair didn't get a scholarship—
she wasn't even enrolled in high school.
What was she going to do when the time comes—
get a recommendation letter from her dad?
After losing the house, could she get loans?   170
Would she inherit her parents' problems
and end up like Charles Dickens, the author
who grew up with his family in debtors'
jail? The world's axis tipped inside of Clair.

She set down her steaming cup of caffeine.
The TV in the next room blared pop rock.
In Clair's head, the stimuli multiplied
together but with a big exponent.
Dawn asked what was wrong.

"We went to bed late—
What's wrong with me? What's wrong with me? God, no!"   *180*
Just the thought of panic made Clair panic.
She knew only one way to deal with fear—
run. Her shoes weren't by the front door, but then
she didn't need shoes.

Dawn blocked the way
and started to freak out, herself. "What's wrong?!"

Full-on vertigo was starting back up.
Clair was caught in a cyclone. The more she
wished for an end, the worse the cyclone spun.
And now other people were watching her.
Dawn called for her mother without leaving   *190*
her guard. Stern, but not put out, Dawn's mom steered
Clair to a couch.

"I need to run!" Clair cried.

"Now that's irrational. Stay with her, Dawn."

Dawn's mom brought back two white pills, space capsules,
and aimed them for Clair's gasping, groaning throat.
Clair tried to sit up and get the pills out,
yet a hand with water led her back down.
She didn't want to spill on the sofa.
And the darkness, heavy, came over Clair.

Chapter 5

Meanwhile, Back Home

Clair's mother organized backyard produce
in banana boxes to barter or
sell at the Burns Avenue street market.
For two days, Clair's parents followed their own
pursuits—gardening, poetry—without
worry. They were their own sailing vessels
for once with their own speed and sure heading.
But now their pursuits felt more like escapes
from the house trouble. Mary—for Clair's mom
had a name—examined early summer's   10
haul: peas, lettuces, purple kale, the herbs.
Peppers and tomatoes weren't ready;
even with longer summers they might not
see enough heat or sun in Minnesota.

A deeper current of thought made tunnels
beneath the hard, sweaty work of gardening—
how would they defend this land from the bank,
and should they try? The bank owned it, in truth.
Every time Mary or Clair's dad, Paul, said,
"Our house," they uttered a lie. A mortgage   20

is rent-to-own—after twice the value
of the property's paid in interest.
And what did "legally" mean anymore?

No cop cars policed the neighborhood streets.
A currency of almost pure barter
meant nobody in East St. Paul carried income
and therefore didn't have to pay taxes.
For this reason, the government was broke.
How would the bank come in here, "the ghetto,"
to reclaim their *property*—not a *house*   30
where a family lived together and ate
food they grew in the garden. How would they
sell such a property after the crash?
And who would move into this neighborhood?

Paul tried to call many times to arrange
some deal, extra time to find employment,
a renegotiation of the terms.

They spoke to him like he was a criminal.
"Do you understand the consequences
of default?"

       Mary stood behind Paul's chair.   40
"Yes, I understand this calamity.
Without our home, we will be cast adrift,"
he said. *What more was there to lose? Their health?*

Years back, Clair's two parents worried if she
was...normal. She was a difficult child.
Obviously intelligent, nothing
escaped her clever, sharp-tongued attention.
How many times she'd said she hated them.
The slightest slurp of one's coffee sent her
out the door, into the woods, gone to hide.   50
Everyone else's kids were dull, simple,
distractible, easier to manage.
They took her to a social worker when
she complained nobody wanted to play
with her. She had no sleepovers at all.
Paul thought about James Joyce's own daughter,
who was brilliant, much loved, and finally mad.

Life brightened when Clair went to school with him
in sixth grade. Not at first. She resented
the other kids' wealth, their name-brand snow boots.   60
But the school was rigorous, and she thrived.
She saw she could outperform the rich whelps.
Tests made tiny Clair sick with anxiousness.
Around the same time she started to run—
her salvation—a vent for sour feelings.
(That is, until she started to place high
and appear in newspapers—more pressure!)
Clair learned she could relax when she saw how
the nice girls looked up to her for being
different, smart, *herself*, a star in school.   70

Then her life changed, her ride to school ended,
and with the news of the house, something broke.

To see her in bed, lost to vertigo,
was more than a mother could comprehend.
Mary hoped this trip to see her classmate
would feel like a nice holiday to Clair.

The last bunch of kale went into a box.

Chapter 6

Escape of the Running Zombie

For a long time Clair couldn't place what room
she lay in or, for that matter, whether
this bed was hers back home. An umbrella
that disrupted thought hung over her head—
not really, but that was how she felt now.
She felt like a miner trapped in her mind!
Some part of her was nonetheless awake
enough to want to find a shaft to climb.
She stared stupidly out the bay window.
The first recognition was a blue jay   10
fluttering from the nest to her mother,
who was pleased her fledgling could fly alone
back to the stick-nest. Life begetting life.
Another recognition: One who is
administered the blowfish's poison
and left to wake in a grave in three days
is called a zombie, proper. Her dad taught
this when they read about Juliet's death.

Dawn entered the picture frame of Clair's sight.
"Oh, I'm so glad you're awake at long last!   20

Do you feel dizzy?"

What's the right word? "No."

"You're out of it. My mom gave you Xanax."
Dawn went on to say her mom took the pills
when Dawn's dad was out of town for whole weeks.
But he had come back home and promised Dawn
he would help Clair, however he could, with
his pull, his connections, his resources.

Later, the two girls walked toward a playground.
No way Clair could run. The zombie staggered.
They watched mothers push their toddlers on swings.   30
Clair remembered the sense of kicking at
the highest point and, for a moment, flew.
Then, Dawn led her to a chain coffee shop
where they ordered frosty, blended lattes,
twenty ounces of sugar, whole milk, ice.
Slowly sipped, the calories started to
bring Clair back to life.

"God, I love these drinks!"
Dawn cried. Clair wasn't much good for talking,
so her friend listed her favorite things:
coffee drinks, the Harry Potter series,   40
field hockey, friends, and boys with spectacles.
After every word, she glanced over Clair's
shoulder to two older guys, quite possibly
college boys, who noticed neither her looks
nor the fact her mortal frame shared their air.

To sip a straw and observe cars pass by
under the sunlight was enough for Clair.
Maybe this easy life was medicine.
She half-heard Dawn's talk and had an image
of a teen wizard who shouts, *Stupefy!*   50

They ambled back, and Clair took a cold shower.
It woke her up some. Then they spent the day
on cold leather sofas watching TV.
Clair moaned refusal against a hip-hop
beach party program "live" in Miami
though obviously from before the crash.
They watched an old, dark movie with Dustin
Hoffman who runs marathons but then gets
tortured by an evil dentist until
the victim escapes, running in PJs.   60
Dawn wanted to change the channel, but Clair
wouldn't let her. They agreed they never
wanted to hear a dentist's drill again.
Clair hadn't seen a dentist in two years.

She had never met Dawn's father before
today. She knew he was a banker and presumed
he'd wear a pin-striped suit, glasses, and come
roughly in the shape of an egg. Not so.
Sporty, he strode into the living room
wearing glasses, but they were designer   70
frames, light green. He had some gray hairs but none
of Clair's own father's deep, downcast creases.

He greeted Clair with radioactive
warmth. "Heard so much about you! Glad you're here!"

Dawn's mom came in, and Clair saw the mismatch.
It was easy to imagine how they got
married when he wasn't a higher-up,
and she was carefree, spritely, and artsy.
Sudden thought: if Clair had stayed at her school,
she would have gone to Dartmouth or somewhere   80
and would've encountered men like him and
found herself in a so-called good marriage,
becoming a semblance of Dawn's mother.
Clair didn't know if this was good or bad.
But she knew she loved grilled BBQ ribs
and hadn't eaten them for years, not since
she had gone vegetarian at eight.
But her body cried for protein now like
pregnant women who can eat two chickens.
Zombies lack the will to say no to flesh.   90

They ate on the gray-tiled back patio
at a long teak table. Dawn's mom relaxed
her uptightness. Clair tried not to pig out.

They heard New York was "the same as always."
Dawn's dad had traveled there by high-speed train.
Clair's parents once talked about her going
to Iowa by rail to visit her
grandparents, but the tickets were pricey.
Apparently, Dawn's dad rode every week.

Finally, Dawn jumped in with her sly voice.   100
"Dad, my BFF here is in a bind.
I thought we might be able to help her."

He sat up with a look of real interest.
"Anything I can do I will pursue."

Clair, the most modest (and anxious) of girls,
shook her head and wiped the sauce off her hands.
"No, no, no, you've all been so kind to me.
I'm just happy to be here eating ribs,"
though the truth was meat, the tearing of strings,
the chewing of pink tissue, didn't taste   110
as good as she'd imagined. It *was* flesh.

But Dawn, equally shy but bold at home,
went ahead and acted as translator.

"I know I can speak for Clair, my close friend,
whose modesty can hold back what she wants.
She told me all about the sad ghetto
where she lives in East St. Paul. It's a slum!
Even there her parents can't make ends meet.
She'll be homeless in the city without
police, safe travel, or adequate work.   120
I'm all for diversity, but we aren't
talking about friends on Sesame Street."

Suddenly, Clair wondered who this girl thought
she was. They were good friends in the classroom,

yet now she was an alien to Clair.
She spoke up. "Actually, it's not like that—"

But Dawn's father held up a hand to stop.
"Now, now, we're here to help. Our good fortune
brings incumbent responsibilities.
Those who've been given much must give some back."   130

Was the big-shot banker that generous?
Clair thought, forgetting her protestations.
Was this a way out? Would they be okay?
Could he help Clair's parents keep their mortgage?
She smiled. Dawn smiled. Even Dawn's mother smiled.

"We wish to extend an offer," he said,
"to stay with us here as long as you need."

The first smile ceased. *What was he offering?*

"I know what you're thinking," Dawn's dad added.
"But I have some clout with the headmaster.   140
Clair, you were a star student and athlete.
The board of trustees may find aid for you."
At that, a broad look of satisfaction
on that patio with its teak—except
Clair didn't want to abandon her folks,
not even for lattes and fine dining.
Where would *they* live when the house had been seized?

Clair tried her best. "Your graciousness really
astounds me. Gosh. God! But I have to say

my parents need me more than you can know.   150
This sounds like hubris, but I'm all they've got.
Still, there might be one wish you could help me with."
She went on to ask Dawn's dad, the banker,
how one could slow or halt the foreclosure.
Speaking so boldly was like chewing tacks.
But maybe this was a heroic chance.

The man frowned deeply. His women turned.

"That's impossible," he said. "Your parents
signed and are in default of a contract.
We lent them the funds for the property;   160
they agreed to pay us back for thirty
years—no, the irresponsibility—"
(Odd, he already seemed to know about it.)

Clair wanted to argue that her parents
weren't responsible—not for the collapse
of home prices in 2008, nor
for the end of oil which took her dad's job.
Instead, she rose, thanked them for their kindness,
and went to find her bike in the garage.
She was embarrassed for having asked him.   170

The three-car slatted door was left open.
Not a bike in sight hanging from rafters
or balanced against the walls.

                    "Clair, don't go,"
Dawn said from behind. "Don't you want to stay

35

with us and go back to school like before?"
And, in a half-embarrassed tone, added,
"Just like Harry going back to Hogwarts."

Clair gave her a hug she firmly felt and
reiterated her real gratitude,
"But I want to know where my bike has gone."   *180*

"We took it to the shop—"
                    "What—?"
                                    "For repairs!"
Dawn didn't know when the pick-up date was.

Once again, the world tilted on its pole.
Nothing worked out right. What was Clair to do?
These spells weren't going away on their own.
They were right, too: homeless in East St. Paul,
her parents couldn't afford a doctor.
Then—a feeling like an elevator
car had fallen a few feet on its own.

Dawn bent to inspect her guest's unmoored eyes.   *190*
"It's happening again, isn't it, Clair?
Please come inside. My dad could take you home."

What to trust, words or feet? Clair remembered
the little pills she'd been forced to ingest.
She told Dawn good-bye and her gratitude
then began her trot down the Candy Land
winding driveway but this time heading out
with shorts, a school t-shirt, and her shoes on.

Clair needed to get home—and then to save it.

She started slow as a racer warms up   200
before the real race has begun, all form,
not leaping forward, gazelle-like. Instead,
the torso and the head stay straight as a mast—
the better to fend off her dizzy spell—
and the action's all in lifting the thighs,
the calves and ankles and feet falling limp,
so toes are placed down first, then lifted up
even before she knows the foot's been dropped.
Rapid lifting, not striding or pushing.
As when a sailing ship carries its speed   210
after days of flat seas and idleness,
the crew rejoices at wild spray and work.
Swells and waves lose their threat and fall behind.

Chapter 7

Fantasies on the Fairways

Although Clair hated golf, she loved running
the courses, especially in late fall
when ball-thwackers had mostly given up
and cross-country season neared its finish.
When Coach secured permission for the runs,
the team could give up neighborhood sidewalks
and the Green Way commuter biking trail—
both boring!—and Clair could take to fairways.
Despite autumnal rains, the course scarcely
got too wet since it was designed to drain.   10
Yes, she hated golf courses, the huge waste
of land and water for a few old guys with bucks.

But now, back on the Hopkins course, heading
toward the cities, she remembered what she
loved most in middle school when she started
to train with the Upper-School team (and win).
In her imagination, she could run
with the elves. She had been reading Tolkien
around the same time and just as she seemed
in others' eyes to find success in school,   20

she really had given up on conflicts
in the everyday world. She held herself
in reserve from normal sixth-grade worries.
So she did her homework without a fuss;
she satisfied her parents' sweet concerns;
with friends, she was kind and low-maintenance,
which proved to be a simple formula
for friendship with almost anybody.

No one knew, except her English teacher
who was privy to what she was writing,   30
that Clair lived this other life in her head
where books she devoured until 1 a.m.
met and mixed past any sense but her own.
Literature was the greatest escape.
Harper Lee's Scout dreamt of Boo in the woods
where she was spied upon by Shakespeare's imps
and fairy folk. To run on a golf course
granted Clair freedom and the relative
scenery to place her in Middle Earth.
There, she could chase after kidnapped hobbits,   40
or bear a message for Galadriel.
A golf course was supposed to imitate
ye olde English countryside, after all.

Yet oddly, with half the world now thrown back
to a pre-oil age—and the foreclosure—
combined with her being three years older,
Clair couldn't sustain her old fantasies.
At best, she imagined a symphony,
lowered her lashes to see through cobwebs

and summoned a gray, melancholy mood.   50
How sharp her feelings used to be back then!
Now she felt either high panic, or zip.
How she envied Dawn with her Hogwarts dreams!

At this point, Clair could find satisfaction
in small doses, small as the well-paced steps
of a distance runner. Satisfaction
only in the fact of them, one plus one,
suddenly equaling ten steps, ten miles.

Clair heard a ball fly by. On the tee box,
a foursome of bastards waved and flicked her   60
the bird. They'd been aiming right at her head!
She ran ahead, caught up with the golf ball,
threw it into the center of a pond.
Thwack! Thwack! Thwack! Three more balls were shot
    her way,
but now she was pulling ahead of range.
She cut through a copse of trees to the next
hole. More golfers carted in the other
direction. Duh! It wasn't fall but June.
Now Clair felt kind of bad (that was her way).
She decided to stick close to the trees.   70

To dodge and to weave brought life to running,
a response to sensory overload:
eyeing trees, stones, variations in ground,
receiving the calls of robins, blue jays,
feeling one's body in movement, content
with each footfall, cool in shade, warm in sun,

dull pain eclipsed by satisfactory
sprint strides. 'Twas, with grace, a meditation.

Clair didn't hear the golf cart behind her.
The driver approached close enough to seize   80
her elbow as one would stretch for a glass.
A natural reaction to such a shock,
the running girl leapt the opposite way.
The man, strong in that surprising aspect
of the obese, didn't release her wrist.
However, a pine came between the two,
and the man's unyielding arm took the blow.
With a shout, the clod tumbled from the cart,
his arm yanked out of the shoulder socket.

Clair thought of kicking the man in the face   90
while he was down and vulnerable. But
he easily could've been someone's dad.
Wry, she said, "I'd ask if you need a hand,
but you still have mine." In spite of the fall,
he did. Again, his face made a target.
Strange, Clair had never thought of violence
except to abhor it. *Peace was a choice.*
The guy let go. He stood, his arm, lifeless.
What a bunch of moaning from a grown man.

"Get in the cart," Clair said. "I can drive you."   100
He looked like Frankenstein in a golf shirt.

"You need to come with me. Boss's orders."

Clair took small steps back to give herself space.
"What's your boss want with a girl on a run?"

The fat man sneered, "You aren't running right now."

She took off, no time for conversation
with the moron who had accosted her.
In the distance, above the trees, she saw
the apartment towers in the city.
The golf course would lead to its own end and   110
its risk would be replaced by another.
Clair's back tended to curve slightly forward,
a bad habit to correct. She straightened.
There was the end, thick brush, someone's backyard.

"The boss still wants to see you," a voice said.
Clair sprinted forward, approached the bushes,
picked her legs up. Where was her fanny pack?

"Wait, Clair!" the voice, now a tad soprano
said, "It's me, Nat! I'm the boss who wants you!"

Chapter 8

Like Kings and Queens

Clair rode in a golf cart with her classmate
from sixth and ninth grade. How Nat had changed.
His mouth and egghead were the same as then,
but his eyes were bigger, contained more brown.
His hair had grown out in boy-band fashion,
belied by his country-club collared shirt.
He hadn't grown much taller but how smooth
he spoke now compared to his old trembling.

"Tony's a fine fellow but quite old-school
when it comes to his duties as warden,"   10
Nat was explaining about the grabby
guy from before. "I sent him to ask you,
nicely, to join me for lunch. I'm sorry!"
One hand gestured above the steering wheel.
He felt free to cut in front of golfers
setting up their shots, not stopping for putts.

"So are you managing this place?" Clair asked.

He explained his father had owned the golf course.
It used to be public in the old days
when Clair had been there with the running team.   20
But the city traded the land for gas,
which Nat's dad had been keeping in storage
tanks as an investment before the crash.
Now he owned acres and acres of land!

A golfer flubbed his sad bunker escape
and scowled at Nat for not having first braked.
"Get off my land," Nat said, "or I'll shoot you."
The poor fellow unstrapped his bag and left.

"That's no way to treat your customers," Clair
said. Nat explained he and his dad didn't   30
plan to run a golf course too much longer.

"Will you sell the land for development?"
"No," Nat replied. That was all he would say.

The cart passed through a narrow corridor
of spruce trees that tunneled a long distance
until opening before a meadow
on a hill. A tall structure dressed in sheets
and scaffolding occupied the hilltop.

Clair asked if it was a water tower
getting a fresh coat of paint?

Again, "No."   40
Nat guided her into an aperture
beneath the tall scaffolding and white sheets.
Inside, only stairs, a spiral staircase.

A runner could train, Clair thought, on these stairs.
They could not speak, for the long tube in which
they rose reverberated with pounding.
Outside, workers placed stones and scraped mortar.
Every twenty feet, slits wide as a gun
let in just enough light to make one's way.

Finally they rose to an iron door.   50
Nat produced a long black skeleton key.
Ker-clunk! Clair tiptoed into a surprise
that really wasn't a total surprise—
a stereotypical teen's bedroom—
that is, a stereotypical boy's.
Somewhere under a heap of clothes and sheets
lay a mattress. Coverless magazines.
Wadded paper balls. Littering a desk,
though, were works of literature Clair loved:
Dante. Old Homer. Whitman. Dickinson.   60
So, Nat got cool but was still a book nerd.

"You're right. This isn't a water tower."
"Indeed," Nat said, "it's my own huge bass tube."
Clair laughed a little.

Nat smiled at himself.
Then he climbed a yellow ladder and shoved
up a hatch. "Come on," he said. "Take a look."
They came to stand on top of the tower.

Clair was fascinated but also scared
to stand at one of the open square cuts
in the battlement. "Why on earth would you—"   70

"You can see all the way to East St. Paul,"
Nat said.
                She couldn't see to the river.

"O Clair, you are a long run from your home.
You wonder why we're ditching the golf course?
Why we're building a medieval tower?
Come on, Clair. You're the smartest girl I know."

Before she could demure, he continued:
"Time is turning back! On many levels.
For one, I got kicked out of school last year.
Had you heard? Let's just say I stretched the rules.   80
Of commerce. You're confused. Let me go back.
Shortly after you left, I blew a fuse.
Probably I'd been blowing them awhile.
Remember how I used to get upset
at late homework? A few points missed? Stray hairs?
Well, I wasn't always a mental case.
I was happy when I was a small boy.
I used to build towers of stone and sand—

but then school overloaded my circuits.
I used to have trouble just breathing out   90
during a lesson where a teacher would
insist we did things the way they wanted.
'Make sure you do this! Make sure you don't—'
Well, in tenth grade I came to a sharp point.
On every rubric, I saw 'Poor.' Poor! Ugh!
One particular paper assignment
led to my pulling out my hair in class.
I'm glad you weren't there to see my crisis."

"Oh, Nat..."

       "Actually, it was all good.
I had to stay home for almost a month.   100
I was given lots of pills to ingest.
Remember 'the stirrings' in *The Giver*?
Hah, hah! These were basically the same drugs.
I felt utterly painless and okay.
Back in school, I saw my own old symptoms
of nervousness *on everyone else!*
I wanted to help, so I sold them meds.
It was a bustling business, let me say.
Again, I'm sure glad you weren't there to see
me become a popular drug dealer.   110
A couple teachers were buying from me.
Here's the weird part: When they apprehended
me, sent me home, banned me from the school grounds,
I achieved my worst-case scenario,
utter failure to follow the guidelines."

A fox appeared between the trees below.
Nat and Clair paused to see it freeze then run.

"*Vulpas vulpas*," Nat said. "So there I stayed,
stuck at home, at the same time you were gone.
What did you do with your newfound freedom?"   120

The fox had disappeared.
                              Clair said, "Not much.
I read library books for every class
and discussed them with my father. Slept. Ate.
I grew vegetables with my mother. Ran."

Nat launched again. "I did more mundane tasks.
I was so destroyed I could do nothing
except sit in our bourgeois backyard
and make towers out of rocks and twigs. See?
Full circle. Time went in reverse for me.
I looked like I was nuts, but I was *glad*.   130
I feel—"
              "What do you feel?"
                                   "Things inside me.
Right as I was regressing, the oil crashed.
Time spiraled back to the pre-industrial.
I saw the trend, and now I'm setting it.
With prices skyrocketing, I advised
my father to trade his holdings in gas—
before everyone moved past needing it—
for holdings in land. The peasants grow food.
Law and order have broken down. Water

will collapse next as deserts travel north   140
with the warming and deforestation.
Who will serve as protector of the realm?
The feudal land owner in his tower."

Nat held out his arms and offered a leer.

Clair looked past him at the swaying treetops,
city buildings in the distance, condos
over Lake Calhoun. It all looked the same
as it used to.

        "And you could be my queen."
Clair laughed.
           Nat frowned. "Is it so unlikely?"
She said, "You wouldn't want me. I'm a mess."   150

Nat lost a bit of his confident tone.
"Well, why not embrace failure and regress?"

What he said was compelling in a way.
The medieval part, not being a queen.

When he reached to embrace her, physically,
though, she put up her hand and said to stop.
He kept coming like a movie mummy.
She reached behind his head as if hugging,
but quickly snapped it down and raised her knee.

He came up bleeding. "Another failure."   160

Sincerely apologetic, Clair said,
"I'm sorry, Nat, but stop being such a creep."

He resumed his triumphant attitude.
"Then you can't be my queen. But I do need
a messenger. You're suited for that work.
You're fast, quite small, and inconspicuous.
Do you know the witch's hat tower?"
He pointed past the city to the east,
across Franklin Avenue's graceful bridge.

Clair knew that tower. Her mother brought her   170
when she was little to play at the park.
Yes, the witch's hat was on her way home.

Nat held out a manila envelope.
"Take this letter. Go to the base and find
Mrs. Smith. Call for her at the bottom."

Clair said, "Why a note? Just send her a text."

Nat led her back toward the trapdoor ladder.
"Too old-school for texts. You'll see what I mean.
It was pleasant to see an old classmate.
I had always thought you were the smartest."   180

Then they progressed from his messy bedroom
down the spiral staircase with no more words.

Chapter 9

Like Father, Like Father

The poet, Clair's father, sat in his room.
His fingers tapped out beats on the desktop,
pentameter being his favorite line.
Paul refused to admit old memories
to the amusement park of his troubled mind.
His own father used to tell him his fears,
how he lived in terror of bankruptcy.
Paul realized that his own adulthood
was the realization of those fears.

Paul's own arrogance precipitated   10
this fall. He used to walk the school hallways
and believe he was the best teacher
in the school, or at least in his building.
He believed he was untouchably good.
What a hollow palace he'd occupied.

Nearby stood a sepia-toned photo
of his Grandpa Hans and Grandma Svanhild,
Norwegian immigrants he'd never known.
The carpenter, Hans, sat in his three-piece

suit, pale-eyed and proud. Behind him she stood,   20
Svanhild, square-jawed and holding large roses.
Paul keenly felt their dream had been let down.
Their descendants—himself, Clair—were worse off
than European paupers who at least
probably owned their cottage and some goats.
Clair would receive zero inheritance.

She'd been gone to her friend's now for three days.

Paul's mindless tapping on the table ceased.
He stood up from the chair in which he wrote.
Time had come to give up on reflection.
He looked out the room's one window to trees,   30
pine boughs that blocked him from seeing further.

Chapter 10

Twilight of the Wannabes

Clair once worried about time and distance.
Now she just ran, and she felt light and strong
though her only goal was to deliver
a note and get home. The Greenway Trail wrapped
like a belt under bridges and across
the stretched waistband of Minneapolis.

She'd had to climb over the golf course's
chain-link fence with a graceful stretch
on top but came down past the barricades
into the city's supposed wastelands.   10
Here, too, as in St. Paul, park lands were turned
into family farm plots, some with small sheds.
Clair wondered if some families lived in them.

Grown men and teenaged boys eyed the runner,
yet her pace didn't give them time to think.

Once she'd passed Lake of the Isles on the left,
the trees gave way to urban concrete gray.
Sometimes she passed little industrial

plants that had gone quiet. An Age, reversed.

To reach the witch's hat tower, she'd traverse   20
the city and then the old Stone Arch Bridge
on Franklin Avenue, maybe ten miles.
Her father used to vary the commute
with different routes to avoid the traffic.
Peeping at the note was a temptation,
but it felt vaguely dishonorable.

How suddenly darkness comes in summer
well after dinner, of which she had none,
only long draughts from still-working hoses.
The sun fell behind trees, and shadows stretched.   30
Trail-sided farmers were packing for the night,
baby strollers and bike carts carrying
a few tomatoes, zucchini, and squash.

Clair's energy level bonked, she slowed down,
let herself walk. Her hips felt like sharp points.

Then, out of the trail's dark edge, five figures
stepped out and circled the exhausted Clair.
Four of them were girls, one boy, pale white teens
wearing all black.

              "She's small, but she'll still bleed,"
one of the girls said. The other girls   40
smiled weirdly. The boy, who was attractive,
Clair noted in spite of herself, held back.

"Hey, I don't have anything worth stealing,"
she announced.

The first girl said, "Just your blood!"

The state of being surrounded at night
on an isolated path by unknown
persons is alarming enough. Panic
should have come to Clair then, as it had come
before. Teens who think they are vampires deserve
even more serious consideration.   50

Rather, Clair felt curious and confused.
"Wow. So you all really think you're vampires?"

The smallest girl, whose lips were balmed black, smirked.
"*He* was the first one. He goes to our school.
We fell in love with him, and he changed us."

The boy held up his hands as if to ward off
blame or credit. "What can I say? *Four* girls!"

Clair, recipient of the writing prize,
took the details and good aim at the boy
and let her story fly:
                      "At last you found me.
How often I lay in bed, sending you   60
telepathic love messages. Take me!
Change me as you changed them!"

55

The boy guffawed
at his luck and his preferred sort of "change"—
the girls desired one *V*, he another.

Clair addressed the girls: "I'm grateful to you
for being willing to share him with me.
What's one more slice out of such a hot pie?"

Each of the girls looked at the boy, weighed him
on some internal scale. Clair didn't move.   70
If she ran, her story would fall apart.
She thought to step forward, present her neck,
but the girls might beat her up, and what if
they *were* vampires?

Finally, one spoke out:
"You haven't earned him yet. You didn't wait
a semester through boring science labs
to see if he'd catch a falling beaker.
You didn't catch him in the woods to see
how his skin glittered in a bright sunbeam."

Clair took this opportunity to say,   80
"Then let me return at the next new moon.
Let me bring you a token of some worth."

The girls were curious. They smiled with greed.
"Sure thing, *sister*. But don't bring anyone."

The boy gave Clair a knowing smile and said,
"Yeah, make sure you come back. Keep it real, babe."
The girls sprang into the night with the boy,
weary, not as springy.

Clair ran again.

Chapter 11

Fire Dances

Clair reached the river boulevard to find
men pushing wheelbarrows with fresh logs.
Under dead streetlamps, Clair ran in shadows
just able to see the river below
in wide gaps where the oaks had been chain-sawed.
Winter preparations started in June.

She crossed the Franklin Ave bridge and looked down.
The river rolled far below and one could
see little white caps where water eddied.
And above, stars had returned to urban   10
skies—one benefit of power collapse.
High rises glowed in the corporate downtown,
since they alone could still afford power's price.
So residents relied on battery
headlamps, candles, fireplaces—and outside,
the moon and constellations newly bright,
Cepheus, Hercules, and Perseus.

Where would Clair sleep tonight—on a park bench?
Under the low bough of a fir tree? Or,

could she run all night and take her chances?   20
To stop seemed more precarious than to run.

The university was an architect's dark
dream of fine stone monoliths and empty
paths, empty not since it was summer but
because hardly anyone could travel there
to study. Presumably classes moved
online and never actually met,
a different kind of ghost town of learning.
Like Dawn, many of Clair's old classmates still
could afford Macalester, Carleton, or   30
take a train east to one of the Ivies.

Far ahead she saw cannibals feasting
on an infant. Closer, she walked and saw
they had been a Japanese maple tree
waving in the wind under the moonlight.
She touched the tree once under its thin arms.
The baby had been a little boulder.

Along University Avenue,
the Chinese restaurants and appliance
parts shops weren't boarded up, just closed, broken   40
windows with faint flickering lighter flames
inside and otherwise vague, dark movements.

Then, in a quick-change act so often loved
by cities, the next neighborhood defied
the previous. Clair turned onto leafy
roads with funky, tight-packed homes, all different.

Candle-lit lanterns hung from tree to tree.
Families sat out front nursing small fires
and glasses of what was likely home brew.
Stone-lined paths led between hostas and yards.   50
In the near distance could be heard singing,
a guitar, obligatory bongos.

If she had to, Clair figured she could ask
any of these families for a bed
and receive safety, a meal, and a roof.
First, though, her goal stood atop a small hill.

The witch's hat tower had its own park.
Its steeple curved over four grand window
openings. Far below was an iron
door, barred and padlocked, and a sign that said   60
it was the highest point in the city,
intended by a Swedish architect
to hold drinking water at high pressure.
Children chased each other around the base,
but there was no Mrs. Smith waiting by.

Clair sat against the foot of the tower.
She fell asleep quite without wishing it,
dreamt of a bonfire and drumming bongos,
masked women and men led by a jester
whose painted face, red and green tri-cornered   70
cap, and rattle came closer and closer.

Chapter 12

Jeremy

Morning rose across Clair's closed countenance.
At first, she refused its invitation.
When she woke, she had the sense of being
misplaced, for she was in someone's hammock
in that someone's neat, foresty backyard
where hostas and artfully placed boulders
lay under oak trees shading a cottage
with its rolling, cedar-shingled roofline,
bulging, stuccoed walls, arched back door, windows.
The place looked like a fairy-tale cottage.   10

Clair loved it on sight and felt green envy
for its owner, who was not to be seen.
Had she somnambulently snuck in here
for a better place to rest her tired frame?
People were even more sensitive to
trespassing on their property these days.
When she sat up, children came out the door,
two identical twin girls holding hands,
and they ran around her just as children
had circled the witch's tower last night.   20

In her half-waking confusion, Clair saw
these high-singing, circling imps in white dresses
and wondered if she had indeed entered
a ring of toad stools like in the stories,
only to be enchanted forever.

Once more, the back door of the cottage came
ajar, and this time a man stepped outside.
The man looked a lot like Severus Snape,
but his nose was bigger and his face thin.
He wore a black t-shirt and holey jeans   30
and looked too old to have two small children,
granted that people in their fifties do.

He asked in an English accent if Clair
wanted some tea or coffee.
                              "Tea," said Clair.

He brought the little girls inside with him
and in six minutes came back out carrying
a tea service—steaming pot, white cups, toast
with butter and marmalade on the side.
They sat at an ornate iron table
on a flagstone patio near a fire pit.   40
A big ashy log in the pit still smoldered.

"We had a late gathering here last night.
On a dare, all of the children raced to touch
the tower up there under the full moon.
They found you fast asleep. A living witch!"
Then the man laughed loudly, maniacally.

Clair almost spilt her hot tea in her lap.

Then the man spoke for a long time without
room for interruption. He was retired
after thirty-five years in a rock band,   50
punk rock at the start, but then heavier.
"We sounded like a thunderstorm over
a volcano erupting. We were loud!
Hahahahahahahahahaha!"

It felt like he was being interviewed.
Meeting a real rock star was exciting
even if she'd never heard of his band.
But he was intimidating, as well,
the largest personality she'd met.

His name, apparently, was Jeremy.   60
He'd been around the world several times
on concert tours. When copy-cat rock bands
made their quick gold and disintegrated,
he kept playing harder and much louder.
Between gigs, he'd conducted orchestras.

"But now the catastrophe I sang of—
our tunes leaned toward the apocalyptic—
after so many years has come at last.
The system collapsed on top of itself.
The great irony is now we can't play.   70
Electricity doesn't work.
We can't turn on our amps. I'm stuck here now

making cucumber sandwiches for girls.
My dream came true, and I'm a domestic man!
Hahahahahahahahahaha!"

He poured himself Taylors of Harrogate
and beckoned for Clair to tell her story.
Strangely, she felt she could trust this rare man,
so she told him all about her attacks,
the foreclosure, Dawn's sort-of betrayal,   80
Nat's message, and her long, foot-bound journey.

"Don't you see? We've all gone primitive now,"
the musician said.

                    "That's what Nat believes."

"Yes, and your friend is banking on power.
Dark-Ages power. But there are older
powers, and these archetypes live in *you*."

Clair knew about archetypes from English.
"Archetypes," she said, "like tragic heroes?"

Wild, Jeremy lit up a cigarette.
"Don't be simple, dear. The old powers are   90
living through you. Gods are living through *you*,
specifically, Clair. The panic you feel
is nothing other than the near presence
of Pan, the goat-god of nature himself.
Cut off from the natural world, humans
forgot the terror of what is most real.

But you've realized it. You've seen the truth."

"So the truth is terrible?"

"To a degree,
certainly. You've seen the maw that swallows
us. Losing your home is but the first loss.   *100*
Ignata Natura Renovata
Integra—nature, when released by fire,
is made whole. You can chew on that awhile."

Clair ate her third piece of toast with orange jam.
"Oh, I think I'd rather not see the truth.
Vertigo is egregious. Fire burns."

"Did it not *end*? Did you not survive, changed?"

"Yes, but I don't want to do it again."

He clunked his tea cup down in the saucer.
"*Want* one. *Will* a panic attack right now!"   *110*

"What?! No way!"

"I promise you it won't work."

Clair regarded his jack-o'-lantern grin.
Then she closed her eyes, pictured the empty
house, her family gone to appease the bank.

"Go ahead," she told herself, "and have one."
She pictured in her mind the future's path
and saw her mother's garden in ruins.
Clair felt a deep sadness, but nothing else.

"You are right. What an irony that is.
To *not* have an attack, I must want one."   120

Then the musician raised his tea to toast
her. She summoned a smile, and their cups clinked.
"Maelstroms will come. Still, we may enjoy our tea."

Clair raised hers to her lips, then halted, puzzled.
"I just remembered waking in the night
to see a party, as you mentioned, but
with the strangest figures. There was a jest—"

"Phantasms of the dream world. But what's real?
Everything has at least two faces, Clair.
Take me—son of mild, British school teachers   130
and trained to play classical violin
but who became a rock musician and
anarchist bent on society's end.
And then I went back to symphonies and
found myself stranded in America,
the father of girls!"

              "Your parents taught, too?"
The musician stepped behind the fire pit,
ashy and cooled yet evocative of—

in a flash, Clair knew *he* was the jester!

A charred stick crumbled with his sneaker's nudge.   140
Behind him, almost hidden in hostas,
stood a small, mossy statue of a faun.

"Yes, perhaps we have a lot in common.
Somewhat curiously, my life has followed
the pattern of the trickster god, Hermes.
And judging by your fascinating tale,
you've been unwittingly serving him, too.
You are a fleet-footed messenger girl.
Along the way, you've dealt out your own tricks.
Going deeper, your young life has been touched   150
by the world of commerce and thievery.
All of these are Hermes's dominions."

"Sir, I happen to be well read in myths,
and I recognize the connection, but
if you're implying my parents are thieves—"

Jeremy approached and knelt at her side.
"Oh, no, please accept my apologies.
The banks are thieves. Usury is thievery.
The Bible says we must give away what-
ever our brother needs without interest.   160
Long ago, I made a mistake. I prayed
for the end of oil, thinking it would
bring down the rest like the fire in Edo,
the great one that consumed the paper walls.
But banks preceded oil, and they survived.

Like your friend, the young baron, they see land
as the irreducible currency.
Luckily, Hermes smiles upon you, Clair,
and he's got resources you can't devise."

Clair couldn't decide if he was mad   170
or had his wires fried from lots of drugs,
but he was fascinating in the sense
she'd never known an adult serious
about a revolution, let alone
live life according to an archetype.

Still, she didn't know what to say or do
in reply. So she took out Nat's letter,
asked the man if he knew a Mrs. Smith.

"Hmm. Where were you to meet her?
The water tower up the path, you say?"   180

He proposed they try to find her up there
and retrieved his twin daughters from the house,
those little beauties like Greek princesses
with trellis-like braids that fell to their waists.

Alessandra and Cassandra said, "Hi."
Both had been painting on small canvasses
some peonies taken from the garden.
Neither wanted to go, but they gave in
at the chance to take turns holding their dad's
black umbrella. No rain clouds coursed in sight.   190

The musician met them outside carrying
a surprise, an automatic weapon,
one with a curved bullet clip like one sees
bad guys carry in so many action flicks.
He and the girls proceeded up the hill
as if they were heading to the mailbox,
armed. Maybe this was a tough neighborhood
after all, in spite of the tiki lamps.

"What's with the gun?" Clair asked.

                        "Makes me feel safe."

"Isn't it a little extreme?" she said.   200

"Who's going to protect us? The police?"

Clair wondered at her own naiveté
and her parents'. She'd gone so far, alone.
Had they underestimated the risks?

By the foot of the witch's hat tower,
they stopped. Clair searched around the paths and oaks
for signs of a Mrs. Smith. However,
Jeremy and his twins stared at the door
into the tower. Using the gun butt,
he made a three-four beat: POUND-pound-pound.   210

"That's not a door for water workers?" Clair
asked.

Click-THUNK. The heavy door swung open.
The padlock and crossbar had been for show!
Nobody stepped out. The man and his girls
gave the door some room; they stood behind him.
What danger would emerge? Mrs. Smith?
Just inside the dark opening there stood
an admittedly elegant woman
maybe somewhere around forty years old,
dressed like a Manhattan fashion model: 220
tall black boots, tights, a buckled jacket-dress-
thing. Her dark hair was long, as was her face,
though overall she had a waifish frame.

"Hi, there. I'm looking for a Mrs. Smith,"
Clair ventured.

          Alessandra spoke up now:
"That's not Mrs. Smith. She is our mother."

Jeremy said, "Clair, please meet Jessica."

Chapter 13

Girl Swap

Jeremy explained how Cassandra and
Alessandra had found the runner, Clair,
sleeping in this very spot late last night.
"She is intelligent, strong, receptive,
and she has a note for a Mrs. Smith."

Jessica was clearly examining
Clair, as if the man sold steaks door-to-door
and she were one of the choicest T-bones.
Clair felt in her small running shorts pocket
and, glad it was still there, offered the note.   *10*

Jessica did not step from the dark door.
Her stare swiveled back to the musician.
"I'm glad for your visit, Jeremy, girls.
You know we could hear your party last night
through the stone walls of the upper chambers.
We'd call the police if there were any."

"Yes, well," he said, "I'm one to wake the dead."
He looked around to see if anyone

71

was approaching where they stood by the door.
He kept his finger in the trigger guard.   20

"As well as the living," Jessica quipped.
"You've always had a gift for catharsis."

He said, "Speaking of gifts, I've brought you one.
If this young woman works out, I want you
to hold back from taking one of the girls.
Indefinitely. Hermes is with her."

The woman rolled her eyes a little bit.

Clair had the start of a panicky spell,
and all of her dreadful symptoms rose up.
She was close to running when he told her,   30
"I think you'll find your parents' financial
difficulties can be solved in this way.
And you'll receive quite an education,
far greater than any prep-school fluffing."

"What are we discussing here?" Clair asked them.

The woman stepped out from the tower door.
She evanesced beauty and confidence.
"We're talking about the Gardening Club."

The musician, gun aimed at the trees, said,
"She means you'll be a witch. They run the world."   40

The Witch's Hat Tower

Jessica turned back to the dark portal.
"Come, Clair. I will take you to Mrs. Smith."

Lured by the chance to help her family,
Clair agreed to follow the witch inside.
The door was shut and sealed with a spinning
circular handle like on a ship's hatch.
The two didn't climb a spiral staircase.
Rather, they entered an old-fashioned cage
elevator. The gate accordioned
shut with a squeak. The witch pressed the button   10
UP. The car rose with a gentle humming.
Clair didn't want to interrupt the sound.

After a long, slow, skyward passage marked
only by electric lanterns, they rose
through a hole in the floor of a round room—
an apartment, really, immaculate,
cool, like a Swedish furniture showroom.
But the elevator car didn't stop.
It lifted through a library, kitchen,

four more living quarters, and finally   20
into what must have been the top level,
a parlor or chill-out lounge with a view.
The large, scalloped windows, Clair realized
were the openings one saw at the top
of the tower, but nobody outside
would guess what was clear here—they were glassed in.

The room was decorated in a style
her parents oohed over: "Arts and Crafts—ooh!"
The vast sofa and armchair were leather;
the lamps were mottled-orange cone shapes, except   30
for the huge chandelier made of antlers
from several elk or moose all tangled up,
lit with fat candles and hanging from high
above in the dark witch's hat ceiling.

Jessica beckoned Clair out of the cage,
who by then felt resigned to her new fate,
acceptance, like one waiting to be hanged.
At the same time (these were complex feelings!),
a strange new kindling lit inside of her
like a stubby candle on the antler,   40
a rather adult cocktail of feelings—
a touch guilty but also eagerness
for what could put her small life behind her.
And, yes, she might end her parents' troubles.

But there weren't any broomsticks to be seen.

The truth was, Clair loved her past with this place.
When still a little girl, her mom took her
on endless walks to while away the days,
and sometimes they used to come around here.
The tower caught Clair's imagination.   50
She thought witches flew out of these windows
at night. This *was* the witch's hat tower.
At the end of one long walk, they ate lunch
at a nearby café that served cupcakes
and soup. She remembered an old woman—
not a creepy witchy one, a prim one—
came to their table and just stared at her.

At last, she turned to Clair's mother and said,
"Oh, you'd better keep a close eye on *her*."
The prim old lady left without eating.   60

Clair's mother said the lady was a witch
from the tower, just playing make-believe.
But Clair couldn't sleep for three entire nights
thinking the witches wanted to get her.

That ancient witch sat in this very room,
occupying the big leather armchair
so unlike the elegant Jessica,
who now stood beside the woman's right side.

Clair's memory was of a long black dress,
but now the woman wore an old-fashioned   70
suit. She stood straight up and was tall and hale.
However, the hand she offered to shake
was an arthritic mass of knobbly joints.
Clair shook it gently, introduced herself.

"Good to meet you, Clair. I am Mrs. Smith."

Startled, Clair gave her the letter from Nat.
She stared out the window facing St. Paul
while Mrs. Smith read.

                          "The young usurper,"
she said, "cannot write a compound sentence.
He hopes to seize the next commodity   80
and the oldest, land. He requests our aid."

Clair asked, "I don't mean any disrespect,
but what sort of aid do you witches give?"

"*Persuasion*," the two witches said at once.

Then, the elder one invited them to
sit and have a cup of tea and some cheese,
a sharp cheddar. Clair tried not to pig out.
Her metabolism was near-nuclear.

"How do you persuade people?" she inquired.

"We use instruments both blunt and subtle.   90
Seduction is Jessica's specialty."
Mrs. Smith indicated her partner.
"In the past, we took majority stakes
in corporations to make decisions.
Still, you'd be amazed to discover, Clair,
our most potent tools. Will you take a guess?"

Clair said, "I thought witches rode on broomsticks.
But you don't seem witchy like that at all."
Then she apologized for her weak guess.

The woman didn't laugh. "Like all legends,   100
the popular conception of witches
is hyperbole. But we're just as old,
and to those aware of our true nature,
we can be feared and hated every bit
as those poor girls who were burned at the stake.
No, we don't use magic or its minions.
Primarily, we write letters. By hand."

Clair waited for more. The woman pointed
toward an unimpressive wooden lap desk
upon which lay a blank sheet of paper   110
and two Uni-ball pens. Mrs. Smith said,
"Surely you have heard the cliché about
squeaky wheels getting oiled?"
                              "Yes."

77

"Well, it's true.
Powerful people receive so little
correspondence that even a few notes
speak loudly, especially if written
with brevity, clarity, fine manners,
yet also a moral intelligence.
Notes don't bear offspring, do they Jessica?"

Quiet, the other woman shook her head. 120

Clair asked if emails would be easier.

Mrs. Smith shook her head, emphatically.
"They are easily duplicated and
and therefore they are mostly disregarded.
But a handwritten note reminds people
of their grandmothers, great-aunts, women
named Florence or Abigail, unknown names
of women one hardly remembers now
except as the senders of birthday cards
who had class, integrity, penmanship. 130
Assistants *pass on* handwritten letters.
In addition, we engineer what we
call synchronicities. You may learn more.
In the meantime, am I to understand
you might join our league of so-called witches?"

Clair explained what she wanted in return.

"In some ways you ask a heftier prize
than a girl who wants her father out

of a death-row lineup. Do schools still teach
Franz Kafka? Have you ever read *The Trial*?   140
It describes an endless maze of judges,
bureaucracies, one person with power
to say, 'I've heard your case and release you.'
Banks work in this way. They don't care at all
what the public thinks because they're faceless.
An entity with no face has no ears
to hear your pleas, no eyes to read letters.
But if you will help execute a plan,
you would demonstrate your aptness to join.
Even banks have appetites to exploit.   150
Do you comprehend? *Your parents would trade
a daughter for a house.* What do you say?"

Clair asked if she could sleep a night on it.

Looking at the empty cheese plate, Smith smiled.
"Certainly. It's the choice of a lifetime."

After a delicious meal of beef stew,
delicious in that way simple meals taste
after long exertion and hunger, Clair
was given a cell phone and asked to text
her parents with the truth: *Hey, I'm okay.*   160
Staying with nice witches (!) who may help us.
Long story. Talk soon.

                    She could have called home,
but it felt right to limit what she said,
at least for now. She was given a room

three floors down like a princess's chamber
except for the Swedish furniture set.

Chapter 15

Elements of Style

The next day a witch assigned her a desk
below a fine view over the river.
The desk was empty except for a cup
with Uni-ball pens and another with
a light-pink hibiscus in clear water.
Her witch's training began with a stack
of letters composed in identical
penmanship yet by different authors
from the last 220 years.
Jessica told her to imitate each,   10
both the penmanship and the writing style,
noun for noun, adjective for adjective,
a verb for each verb, but to change the theme.

"Can you tell me what I should write about?"
Clair asked.
              "It doesn't matter," Jessica
replied.

              The first model was to Lincoln
in 1862, written by one

Sarah Blackwell of Manhattan, NY.
Sarah and her "circle of female friends"
were weeping at the carnage of the war   20
but also that the president had not
stood up against slavery, "our nation's
plague, which slowly rots and reeks our conscience."

Clair addressed her imitation to her
last PE teacher, who had noxious gas.
This version excoriated him for
reckless consumption of antipasto
and that his gas "gradually sickens
and corrupts the students." Pretty childish,
she knew, but that was how she started out.   30

Overall, she found nineteenth-century
letters to be astonishing for their
big vocabulary and metaphors,
but also because by today's standards,
they sounded steamy and dreamy with lust.
Girls wrote to each other with stuff like this:
"O, I long for the lightning flash of touch"—
and that was written by President Taft's
wife to a witch she'd met the week before!

Clair's morning felt like copying love notes,   40
though the intent of each one was to push
some powerful man in a direction.

One dropped a hint to Teddy Roosevelt
to start a system of national parks.

A secret message to Winston Churchill
warned of the rising influence of Hitler.
Letters against nuclear proliferation,
apartheid in South Africa, ozone
depletion by aerosol cans, and more
recently, deep-sea oil exploration—   50
Clair read through dozens of model letters.

The witches—she didn't yet know their name—
wrote with an old-time politeness that almost
sounded British. At the same time they judged
faults with the blunt, flat side of a hammer.

"Sir," one letter by *the* Mrs. Smith read,
"I find Honeywell's willingness to build
electronic components for missiles
an evil stimulated by sheer greed.
If one errant missile kills civilians,   60
my hands are bloody since I pay taxes."

Clair was surprised that witches paid taxes.

Over a lunch of baguettes, herbal tea,
fine cheeses, and tomato-basil soup,
Clair met four other women, young and old,
who lived and wrote out of the hat tower.

Just as school girls spoke loudly at lunchtime,
the witches were chatty after writing.
A curly-haired woman named Margaret
had been printing copies of a pamphlet   70

83

about making backyard gardens friendly
to wild animals and birds. An artsy
girl, not much older than Clair, named Anna
was writing flyers against gas hoarding
in suburbs. A thin old black woman, who
ate with slow care and was named Mrs. Jones,
apparently was a strict editor.

Anna whispered, "Her marks are in sad girls' blood."

There was a middle-aged woman named Sue,
trained as a social worker, who researched   80
irrefutable facts to help writers.

Jessica came in, wet from the outside,
where a storm had arrived over the night.
If anything, she was *more* elegant
with her sodden hair pulled over her ears.

"Oh, you poor drowned mouse. How was the mission?"
Mrs. Smith asked.
                    "A success, as always."
Then Jessica ate in silence, quickly.

Clair wanted to get to know the others,
who called her "the new girl," or "messenger,"   90
but she had lots of questions for old Smith.

"Do the powers-that-be know these letters
come from a single organization?"

Mrs. Smith was making a small sandwich
with a baguette and three-year-old Gouda.
"No. You'll notice we use hundreds of mail
boxes around the world as addresses."

Clair felt so edgy, she grinned as she spoke.
"How do you know letters are effective?"

"We've always led minds in our desired
direction, albeit gradually."

100

"In a way, you're teachers."

            "Ah. Perceptive."

"Do you witches marry? You're a Mrs."

"If marriage suits our purposes, we do.
But we just call elders *Mrs.*, as well."

Clair sunk her spoon in her tomato soup.
"What if I decide not to join you all?"

The lunch-time chatter ceased. The girls sat straight.
Mrs. Smith kept her matter-of-fact tone.
"Then you would go home."

            "I *can* keep secrets,"   110
Clair said. It was true. She was rare in that
she felt no compulsion to vent knowledge.

Looking around for something, old Smith said,
"It wouldn't matter. No one would believe.
Where is that smoked ham? Work demands protein!"

Clair asked, "So why did it get so quiet?"

"They're surprised," Jones said. "No one *wants* to leave."

Anna piped up: "We hate delivery!"
Everyone laughed but Clair, who was confused.

"It's true," Smith said. "Without the mail service,   120
a fleet-footed Mercury is a must."

Anna said, "So go easy on the cheese!"

Mrs. Jones showed up at Clair's desk and sat
primly, back straight. She examined the new
batch of letters and, her voice flat, neither
scolding nor encouraging, she listed
Clair's errors.

                    "See this? A semicolon
separates two independent clauses
or items in a list that have commas.
What you've done here is place it between *fat*,   130
flatulent, and *vulgar*. That doesn't work."

She picked at points like a crane for two hours.
Obsequious, Clair looked at Jones's

fingernails when she pointed at the words.
They were long; strong; pearly, but not quite white;
and shaped like shovels, which interested
Clair for the lesson's full two hours. Meanwhile,
she learned more about the work of writing
sitting with the editor than in all
her English classes or studying with   140
her dad. Learning from one's parents is hard,
if not impossible in the long run.
But monotonous Mrs. Jones was not
there to nurture or to show off for Clair,
so the only thing to be done was learn
though it felt as if each of Clair's eyebrows
were being plucked out.
                     At last, Mrs. Jones
put the stack down and said, "Now that you're done
with this exercise, Mrs. Smith would like
you to deliver a message, briskly."   150

At that point, Clair was given back her gear,
her athletic shoes and shorts, running shirt,
all washed and smelling fresh. She also got
a mesh vest that held two water bottles
and, for letters, a satchel on the back.

"If ever you are attacked, run away
at top speed—the best defense," a note advised.

Chapter 16

Her First Mission

Clair, now mysterious messenger girl
to strangers, emerged from the hat tower,
shot out running in her excellent gear—
not a sparrow or swallow who flew
from point to point, but a willow arrow
who'd been shot from the bow of those witches
toward Minneapolis's skyscrapers.

She saw the IDS Tower written
in the address, slowed her rapid-footed
pace only for the revolving door and to stand   *10*
in an elevator, all the way up,
which opened onto the dark oak paneled
reception area for a big bank's
elite offices and boardroom. A guard
and a secretary looked up, bemused
to see the small, sweaty, hard-breathing girl—
nothing official about her, for sure.
But she presented the envelope and
said, putting on her storytelling side:

"I'm a courier with an important   20
dispatch for the eyes of your CEO.
The sender wishes no one else to see
its contents." Clair knew it was a bit much,
but the words came out as they did like dice.

"And who should I say the dispatch is from?"

"Whom," Clair corrected. "I don't know who wrote
it," which was the truth. "But it's important!"

Both of the gatekeepers looked skeptical.
What was a synonym for *important*?

"Trust me, nobody sends a courier,"   30
Clair said, "unless it's for a *vital* cause.
Do you need me to take it in myself?"

The secretary declined her offer.

As Clair entered the elevator and
turned to the shutting doors, she saw men step
out of the reception's far side, all men
in blue suits. At the center was Dawn's dad.
The elevator doors closed before he
saw his daughter's friend. On the long ride down,
Clair wondered if the message was concerned   40
with her purpose for joining the witches.

Downstairs, she looked for a water fountain,
filled one of the sports bottles she'd carried,
gulped down two deviled eggs wrapped in plastic
and placed in her backpack by who-knows-whom.
How long would it take before she would call
herself a witch?
           Under the breathless sun,
she began her run back at a seven-
minute-mile pace, half a minute or more
slower than the speed she took to get there.   50
The letter-writing felt a bit like school,
but running—as a job!—felt like a snow day.

At an intersection with four red lights,
a voice cried out—from where?—"Clair! Clair! Please wait!"

She stopped and saw the source: her dad, his head
sticking out of the driver's side window
of the family's long-gasless Ford Taurus.
He was stopped at a green light while cars honked.

Clair approached her dad. He reached to open
a door. She got in, and he drove ahead.   60
He looked wan and lined from worry and
obvious sleeplessness. Clair felt awful.

She apologized over and over
for having been gone so long. Imagine
the terror of a parent whose teenaged
daughter has left home and then disappeared.

Her father explained that after four nights
since she'd departed, they got in contact
with Dawn's mom who claimed Clair had run away
after some kind of episodic fit.   70
They hoped she would appear on the doorstep,
but when she didn't with a fifth evening
coming near, her father walked to St. Paul
and sold some gold cuff links inherited
from his grandfather. The man in the pawn
shop gave just enough for a tank of gas.
He'd driven the routes she might have taken
until he got to Minneapolis,
downtown, and happened to see her running.
"And what did that text message say? *Witches*?"   80

Clair apologized again and teared up.
She realized he looked like the spirit
of the man who used to take her to parks
all summer long and then brought her to school,
his prestigious school, his gift to her,
and had proudly seen her at every race,
assembly, and awards ceremony.

When she was eight, she had a fervent faith
in God and spoke to the sky and felt heard.
Once, she'd prayed on her knees to win a race,   90
and she did win. She'd prayed to survive exams,
which always turned into the highest grades,
and she'd even accepted the cliché
things happened for a reason and turned out.

She was past that notion now. Beside her
sat a good man, her own father, ruined.

It was only because she had no hope
that she was able to stop crying and
say, "Dad, if I don't do what I'm doing,
which I cannot explain since I do not   100
understand it, then I think I'll collapse.
The world will spin so fast, I'll fly right off.
I'm without hope, so I'm taking a course
of action that is so ridiculous,
but the only way I see I can help."

Her father looked surprised and then horrified.

Clair clarified, or at least she tried to.
"I'm not selling my body if that's what
you think. No! Actually, I kind of am.
Oh, gosh!" She explained a basic but true   110
set of facts. She was delivering mail
for an old woman and her female staff
of writers. And they were teaching her skills,
grammar, rhetoric, better handwriting!
Her situation sounded pretty good
when she described it so.

                              Her dad relaxed
somewhat as he drove University
toward St. Paul. "Can I meet your employer?"
he asked.

At first Clair thought she should say no,
but then thought, *Why not?*—except for the weird 120
point of their residence in the tower.
In any case, she knew how relieved she
would feel if her parents knew she was safe—
even if she *wasn't* going to be.

She had her father pull up at the park.
He hunched as he walked just as he sat, bent
at his desk reading *The Complete Shakespeare*
with no students to teach the plays to now.
Would he recognize Mrs. Smith and Jones,
and Jessica as *Macbeth*'s three witches? 130
Would he recognize Clair, for that matter,
as Ariel, the faerie girl who went
everywhere she wasn't supposed to be,
and himself, her father, as old Prospero?
The big splurge of every autumn and spring
used to be to see every production
by the Bard with teacher tickets from the
Guthrie Theater. Magic made human,
the plays had cut Clair free from reality.

Rather than having to bring Dad upstairs, 140
Mrs. Smith happened to be sitting there
on a park bench observing the sun fall.
She looked, as before, like an old teacher,
in her skirt, suit coat, and ruffled white shirt
one of the schoolmasters who used to run
an entire schoolhouse of all ages.

Her father recognized her as a peer
though they'd never met. He even looked pleased.

"You have a remarkable daughter," Smith
said in that way of teachers who'd never   150
praise their students so much as when parents
were around. "Would you mind, sir, if we help
develop her obvious, fine talents?
I understand she isn't attending
her former school. Clair ought not go to waste."

Clair's dad pulled at his ear. "Yes. I agree
completely. But will you take care of her?"

Mrs. Smith's ramrod-erect deportment
standing tall by the bench contrasted with
Clair's stooped-over father.

                        "Take care of Clair?"   160
she said. "I should think so. We'll feed her well,
provide her with friendship, a warm room—and cheese.
She will be educated to a life
in letters. We have a desire to keep
her fit. She will visit home when she can,
which may not be as often as you'd like.
But we know your daughter is no orphan,
that she's loved, and we'll try to do the same
in loco parentis. At age eighteen,
she can choose her own path as she would like."   170

"Like an old apprenticeship?" Clair's dad asked.
The question told Clair he was buying in.

"Yes," Mrs. Smith said. "In the oldest sense."
With that, she offered him her knobbly hand.
Then Clair hugged her father and kissed his lips
like she did when she was a little girl
getting tucked into bed. She watched him drive
toward St. Paul and home where he'd tell her mom.

Clair rode up the elevator car with
Mrs. Smith. "I delivered the message,"   180
was all she said between the passing lights.

They both faced the cage door. "You have a kind
man for a father," Mrs. Smith told her.

"Thank you, ma'am, for putting his heart at ease."

Mrs. Smith croaked a little. "Certainly.
I've spoken to hundreds of girls' fathers.
Although the orphans *are* more cut and dry,
I did mean what I said."

                    The car halted.

Chapter 17

Synchronicity

For the first time in weeks, life felt normal
though of course it wasn't normal at all.
It was life—now with a direction.
Mornings, Clair practiced writing from letters
as Mrs. Jones edited her to shreds.
And afternoons she ran deliveries
which always came in time, for the mental
strain of writing made her feel dizziness,
not whirling, but a little lightheaded
again. She didn't tell anybody,   10
didn't need to; whereas her vertigo
used to terrify her, making it worse,
now it was merely an unpleasant fact.
The trick was not to get over-aroused.
It went away when she started to run
unless she got dehydrated, bonky,
but that was different and why she carried
the water bottles for her longer trips.

She often went between the two downtowns
with correspondence to someone's office,   20

the much-diminished mayor, whomever.
She took notes to local Somali groups
in Minneapolis and Hmong leaders
in St. Paul and sometimes between the two.
She crossed the great river four times a day.
Clair didn't see the content of the notes,
yet she was sure some alliance was in
the works between the groups she visited.

Anna, who turned out to be Clair's roommate,
chatted, practically to herself, each night   30
with Clair playing the patient listener,
which was fine with her. Anna told how her
own mother had been one of the witches,
but she'd never known her well, or her dad.
All the time she listened, she pet a cat
named Tug who caught mice in the tower walls.
Clair learned a lot from the nighttime chit-chats.
The true name of the witches was really
The Highland Ladies Garden Society
though it didn't refer to Highland Park   40
in St. Paul, but a much older "Highland."
They liked to think of themselves as gardeners,
not witches, which was derogatory.

In fact, they were ancient. Women had been in charge
before the later militaristic
societies formed. Then religions changed.
Hunting gave way to farming, which in turn
brought new male gods who led with scythes, not bows.
Now, agriculture could sustain armies

97

intended to conquer newly plowed lands.   50
Greek, Roman, and Chinese women and girls
were essentially locked away to weave,
to work the looms, to fret over men's fates
in an age when husbands could be slaughtered,
and the women would be made into slaves.
So they took matters into their own hands.
Shut away in their dark rooms, they began
to whisper ways to influence events
for the better. Men never suspected
they met to do more than gossip and sew   60
though some guessed and cursed at the power of wives.

In modern times, the Society held
large sums of money, which they used to buy
politicians, large voting blocks of shares
in companies, education for young
members, nursing for older ones, as well
as towers. These came to be a symbol
that stuck, especially empty water
towers which they fashioned into covens.

Anna, a gabby chatter to rival   70
Dawn at bedtime, played hide-and-seek behind
her pillow one night. "You'll never guess what
I did today," Anna said and then hid.

They wore identical, long, white nightgowns,
Garden Society standard issue.
Clair smiled a little but didn't say she
had *not* noticed or wondered about her.

"I won't guess," Clair said. "But you can tell me."

Anna's head reappeared; her eyebrows arched.
"I took a long walk to the train station.   *80*
You know, walking? Easier than running
and a helluva a lot less sweaty, girl."

Clair replied, "Why did Mrs. Smith have you
deliver a message instead of me?"

Anna swiped at Clair's head with her pillow.
"You think you're so special! I've got legs, too."

The cat leapt down to begin his night work.

"Come on. What were you doing at the train
station?"
       "We-ell, I had to find this guy...
Really, I shouldn't say. Secret mission   *90*
and everything."
         "Why did you mention it?"

Anna practically stood up in her bed.
"Because it involved you! At least your name—"

Clair sat up on her own, eager to know.
"Then it *is* my business. Tell me, Anna."

Anna hid behind her pillow again.
"Actually, I'm feeling rather peckish,

whatever that means. Time to go to sleep."

Clair walloped Anna's head with her pillow.

"Oh!" Anna cried. "You're victimizing me!"   100
Whomp! Whomp! Anna laughed deliriously.
Whomp! on the unprotected midsection.
Anna lowered her pillow. "You little—"

"Are you going to tell me now?" Clair cried.

Anna propped up on one arm and lifted
her own pillow with the other before Clair
reached out and pulled the propping arm away.
Grimly satisfied, she felt her small, light,
muscular body was capable of
surprising cruelty. "So what happened then?"   110

"Okay. You win. I need to start running,
too, but I doubt I ever would want to.
The facial expressions of runners say
it all. You should see yourself sometime, Clair."

Then Anna's eyes squinted with discernment.
"I'd been given a picture of a man.
I had to locate him and walk close by
while pretending to talk on a cell phone.
Then I had to say, loud enough for him
to hear, 'Oh, my friend Clair will be homeless   120
soon—' and by then I was well past the man.
Don't you think it's about you? Why on earth?

You're not homeless. You live with us now, here."

Clair sat back down in a chair by the bed.
She asked for a description of the man.

Blue business suit. Fit. Designer glasses.

Clair said it was the father of a friend,
Dawn's dad, the banker. It seemed the gardeners
were applying pressure in her favor.
Were they pulling out weeds, or planting seeds?   130

Clair sat still. "Why would they have you walk by
and say that? Is it to intimidate him?"

Now Anna stood up straight, like Smith, taking
the role of lecturer. "I have so much
to teach you, you newb. It's one of our old
methods of persuasion. Later, a guy
named Jung coined the term *synchronicity*.
He was talking about coincidence,
how you might hear the same word—I don't know,
like *bumblebee*—three times in a day and   140
then you get stung walking barefoot outside.
Maybe there's something magical to it.
Jung said they were meaningful connections.
Or at least people put them together
in their heads. Mrs. Smith says the human
mind longs for connections, and we *use* them.
We'll plop down a suggestion—like 'Help Clair'—
in different ways surrounding a person.

The first touch, usually a letter,
is really clear to get it on his mind.   150
Then we drop names or pamphlets with the word.
Subtle little pings of recognition."

Clair said, "I've always liked the word *subtle*."

"Yeah, I know, but it's spelled weirdly. SUB-tle.
It must be French with its silent letters.
Anyhow, I guess the Society
wants this guy to think about you a lot."

Clair folded herself back into her bed.
She stayed up late with Anna rambling on
with frivolous stories about how she   160
once snuck into Jessica's chamber, which
was normally locked but wasn't this day,
and her drawers were filled with black lingerie!
"It was like a Victoria's Secret!"

Clair declared, "You have an immoral mind."
Then she realized *she* sounded like Smith.
At the same time, she still was thinking on
what Anna had said before and whether
engineering coincidences was
an evil manipulation. It *could*   170
cross a line and add up to implied threats.
Certainly the Gardeners messed with folks' heads.
Oddly enough, Clair wasn't sure she cared.
Tug strolled through, this time on patrol for mice.

A darkened house
not part of a neighborhood
alone in dreamland
Clair in ghostly nightgown
searches the backyard
vines consuming the stucco   180
she forces the back kitchen door
to find a wasteland of broken tile
mildew smells and green-stained
sink she crosses the living
room down the hallway dark
as a sexton's hole lit by moon slit
the familiar bathroom where
her mother bathed her long ago
a broken mirror gutted toilet
out of the shadowed corner   190
emerges a witch a real witch
old bent bony crooked long
nosed in all black she says
Here is your lesson girl
you will lose your home
you are not alone
everyone will lose
his home or theirs?
singular or plural
which is correct?   200
For some reason Clair
cannot reply she flies
nightgown stretching long

as a wedding dress
back through the hall
out the kitchen door
into her mother's garden
where more witches
dig themselves out
of the garden beds 210
Clair runs and runs
looks back to see
though she knows she
shouldn't look back
the jade plant
like an ancient god
grown big as a tower
glossy leaves like
licks of flame.

Chapter 18

The Engineer of Hope

Those books that stood out best in memory
were those Clair learned in her last English class,
though she had read many since, on her own,
and those her father pulled from his bookcase
to glean in the fullest sense of homework.
So now, running on her umpteenth mission,
her mind held conversations with characters
from those ninth-grade texts.
                         Thus, Atticus Finch
interrogated her; his voice was deep: 10
You sure did a lot of running that day.
Let's see. You say you ran up to the house,
you ran to get the sheriff. Ran again...

"Yes, yes," Clair breathed. "I'm running the whole day!"
Her quadriceps, her shoulders, and her feet
all joined in chorus: "O! How we're punished!"
The air had grown cool, and the sky turned dark.
A Minnesota summer can forget
itself in this way, reminding one that
the sun's gift was only given on loan

So Clair pushed her body harder, her legs   20
to pump faster, for it was capable.
If she could reach the river boulevard
and cross the Franklin bridge's elegant
span before heaven above spilt on her,
then she could nearly sprint the final mile
to the tower and dry sanctuary.

The day was buoying her anyway
with hope. She'd delivered some documents
Mrs. Smith had insisted reach the hands
of the new council leading the Calhoun   30
Beach Club, a playful name for residents
who lived around the Minneapolis
lakes. They used to be wealthy liberals,
but Clair just saw white-armed people in soiled
coveralls at a park for dogs off leash.

They listened to a Polish guy explain
how one could build an "open-source roto-
tiller" from spare car parts. The old lady
who received Clair's sweaty envelope plopped
it near a half-built chicken tractor and   40
cared more about the hydraulics involved
with lowering the tilling plate gently
so the whole machine didn't break or flip.
Clair stayed the while and marveled how quickly
these people had changed their entire lives.

When the arc welder began suddenly
to smoke, Clair figured the work was kaput,

but the Pole fished inside and found a mouse
who had been zapped. He tinkered with the tool—
everyone appreciated his skill—   50
until the arc was crackling again.

Apparently, Milocz, the Pole, traveled
city to city in a modified
train he'd built out of disused railroad cars,
a caboose he lived in, an engine that
was powered by body waste, as well as
two cattle cars that bore his inventions.

Tall and bearded, he looked like any young
mechanic. He asked the crowd, "Do you want
to see the backhoe built out of a Jeep?"   60
But when another train blew its whistle,
the Pole cried out, "Dammit! I didn't know
the track I'm parked on would be so jammy!"

He started running toward Lake of the Isles.
Everyone followed him, including Clair,
who ran so fast, she caught up to the Pole
and passed him, flagged down the oncoming train,
which fortunately had been moving slow
through the city limits and braked up short.

Milocz told Clair, "Thanks! I'll never create   70
a machine to match those fast feet of yours."

The engineers of the just-arrived train
crawled down from their ladders bearing shotguns.

"Let us pass by," one barked. "We will fight back
if you think you can raid us for booty."

They pointed their weapons at the Pole who
stood there, scruffy and holding a wrench.

Clair, the innocuous girl, stepped forward
and explained the travelling invention
show.

    "Vulcan Open Source Engineering!"   80
Milocz said.

       The train engineers relaxed.
"Forgive us. We've been raided more than once.
When families starve, folks grow desperate."

They told of changes across the landscape.
Farms on the Great Plains were becoming vast
estates made rich by the high cost of food.
Cities, on the other hand, went two ways:
Those like Birmingham and Baltimore fell
to destruction, chaos, fed by old rage
that had been held in check by the police.   90
But some, such as Portland and Cleveland, still
survived, even turned greater than before
the fall of oil.

       Milocz agreed. "Yes, I
have seen the same. Where some equality

and a decent living had existed,
now they've become like the Greek city-states.
But the suburbs are collapsing without
fail. They are bilked for food and making none."

The engineers were happy to help load
the Pole's machines into his own freight cars.　　　　　100
They praised his do-it-yourself devices.
The Calhoun Beach Club received free designs
on a DVD.

　　　　　"Send me an email,"
Milocz said, "if you have any problems!"
He turned to Clair. "How can I thank you, miss?"

She decided she could trust this man, asked
for a ride east until the train tracks bent
north. How delightful, climbing up the rungs
of this private train's ladder into the
engine with its revolving satellite　　　　　110
TV dish and side panels welded from
car hoods. The interior was crowded
with laptops, smoothie blenders, and a Lay-
Z-Boy aimed toward an instrument panel.

A golden, furry ball in a small cage
ruffled, two eyes blinked, and what emerged from
newspaper litter was a hamster who
climbed his wheel. As he began to rotate
it, a record player likewise started to
turn—and punk rock played, albeit slowly.　　　　　120

Milocz engaged a throttle, and they rolled
ahead, not without a certain odor.
Then he worked controls on his computer.
"Please excuse my baby's obvious fault.
When her fires light up, the fumes smell like shit."

Clair laughed. The Pole sat down in his chair and
said, "You don't seem like American girls."

She replied, "I'm a messenger. That's all."

He yanked the whistle cord and then increased
the speed. Clair perched beside the right window.   130
Leafy branches brushed and scraped the train's sides.

More screeching and bass pounding emitted
from the record, which played close to the right
RPM as the hamster charged headlong.
The album sleeve was near at hand, so Clair
looked closer. Wearing a weird bowler hat
and standing before his band and a clock
was a much younger-looking Jeremy!
Same hawk nose, same caterpillar eyebrows—
his eyes were wild then, just as they were now.   140
Milocz gave Clair a smoothie "with chia."

"Do you think," Clair asked, "that the Twin Cities
will go the way of Baltimore, or more
like Portland?"

The engineer scratched his beard.
"It depends how dependent you all are.
The comfortable are the vulnerable.
Since the Industrial Revolution,
everyone left everything to experts—
food, medicine, how to build their machines,
even how to play music and to sing.   150
We became like children who need Mommy.
Now she has gone away." The Pole looked down
and pensive for a minute. He continued,
"But those good people today were clever
about many things. Are there more folks like
them?"

Clair thought of her parents and said yes.

"Be glad," he said. "A renaissance has come!"

When they slowed before the north branch line bent—
the grain silos empty, rusty, above—
Clair leapt from the lowest rung, and she ran   160
while waving at the engineer of hope.

In two blocks, industry gave way to homes,
and she ran feeling glad as she conversed
with her ninth-grade books. Then the sky grew bleak.
The heavens spilt before she reached the bridge.
When lightning boomed near enough to startle,
Clair made for the marquee of a movie
theater called the Riverview where she

once viewed a *Lord of the Rings* marathon.
The wind started to whip rain hard sideways. *170*
In one of the pockets of her mesh vest
was tight-packed a poncho she unwrapped
to discover not a plastic hood but
foil meant to contain one's ambient heat.
Anything was better than her wet clothes.
Inside, through the glass doors, Clair could hear loud
music, dance music, and a light glowed blue.
She pulled at the door, and it was unlocked.

Chapter 19

A Vampire Danse Party, Baby

Inside, the music pounded like the noise
under a highway overpass, which Clair
knew well from getting caught in earlier
showers. The lobby chairs were the same sleek
red hipster-era antiques she recalled
except the vinyl had been slit open,
so the fluffy batting was disemboweled.
The black tile floor was sticky from soda-
pop spills. The air smelt like it was freshly
hot buttered but also weirdly smoky   *10*
along with some other scent—sour milk?

The thudding bass became laser-gun bleeps.
Clair started moving toward the theater
doors when a teen girl appeared from behind
the curling panel around the entrance
to the ladies room. She didn't look shocked
to see a stranger, Clair, standing in foil.

"Oh, I so love this! Where did you snag it?"
said the girl, wearing neon bracelets and

necklaces over a boy's V-neck tee   20
plus jeans ridden with holes and sagging down
despite a studded belt. The girl yanked hard
on both double doors at once to reveal
a dance party, a rave, in the movie
hall. Some twenty girls were bouncing, arms raised.
Curious, Clair followed the first inside.

The theater speakers blared at full blast.
A random, rough-cut montage of film clips
blinked, flashed on the screen, unrelated films—
children playing in a daddy daycare,   30
orcs raiding Helm's Deep in the rainy night,
a man who held the reins of a huge worm,
a yak hacked up with a machete blade,
one couple after another made out,
and in between them, colors, lights, black screens
roughly cut, spliced, so she could see Scotch tape.
Clair wondered if this was a type of fun
that she had entirely missed out on.

Everyone looked somewhere around her age.
All seemed to appreciate her foil cape,   40
or they were welcoming Clair's arrival,
for the crowd began to blob around her.
A new, catchy jungle break-beat began.
Oddly, Clair could not help but join the bounce.

A dissonant man's voice began to sing,
Therein are centaurs and now Priapus
with Faunus. The Graces have brought her cell...

To rub and jostle against the bodies,
no matter they were girls and as sweaty
as Clair—now two-hundred degrees within   50
her foil—she experienced a tribal
togetherness that was ecstatic joy.

At first the boy, the handsome boy, did not
stand out though he was the only figure
not dancing in the throbbing theater.
His eyes approached in strobe-flash stutter-stops.
He reached out and held Clair's wrists, not tightly,
so she could still groove, shake her limbs, and move.
He leaned forward and with the softest voice
whispered words she could not distinguish but   60
for an ear-tickling creek of lovely sound.
His pull into the corridor between
the curtains did not get a fight from her.
O! This was the fuss everyone had made
of romantic love! Clair was breathing hard.
A mouth can hunger for another mouth!

His hair, dark and god-like, spiked beautifully.
His t-shirt showed off his arms, lean and buff.

"Forgive me please for interrupting your fun,"
he said. "It's just, I think you are so cool.   70
The other girls in there are nothing like
you. How do you keep oh-so-fine? *For real!*
The stars don't know a light as bright as yours.
But wait. I fear I've made myself too bold

with a nice girl like you. Let me find you
a token, something small, to demonstrate
my good, well-meaning faith. Wait here, okay?"

Clair grinned and nodded. Before he rushed off, he froze
to regard her one more time and smile, sweet.
She said, "What's your name?"

                     "You can call me Troy."   80
Then he was out through a gap in the dark
red curtains. Clair sighed beneath the exit
sign light and tried hard to recall his fine face
she'd seen clear in the strobe-flashed theater.
She felt she'd seen him before, or at least
knew the Platonic idea for Hot Boy.
For that matter, how close the boy's fine speech
echoed lines she knew from Romeo's moon-
and-pilgrim bit from Shakespeare's famous play.
Did he presume she hadn't read the Bard?   90

The beat from the theater then slowed down
to a staccato rhythm with silence
between fence posts of thuds in which Clair heard
a baby's high cries. She parted a split
in the red curtains and found a brightly
lit staircase leading up a flight somewhere.
She tried not to make noise on the steel steps,
but the baby's crying climbed in spirals.

The stairs opened onto a long, narrow
room that was lit softly except for the old   100

film projector flashing its images.
A crib was parked beside a beat-up couch.
A naked baby cried from a stroller.
On the couch lay a sleeping, smallish teen—
no, no, her eyes were half-closed as though drugged.

Yes! Clair knew her—she was one of those girls,
the vampire teenagers who nearly
jumped her. Underfoot, rolled-up, snowball-sized
white diapers made a foul, fruity odor.

Suddenly Clair knew Troy: the vampire boy!   110
He'd just ignited her heart a minute
ago. Shoes pounded up the metal stairs.

Clair had never gone back to find the gang
with a valuable prize on the last full
moon. If they recognized her, they'd get pissed.
Clair did what she did best. She ran fast.

A door at the room's end required all
her effort to budge.

                    "Why did you come here?"
the boy said behind her. "You've ruined it.
You were gonna be different than this mess.   120
You're so much better than these clinging girls.
I understand now what a vampire is!
I gave my life away to foolish games!
Now they suck my life away, this baby,
the girls! I wanted *us* to be wholesome.

117

But I should know nothing's ever as great
as any of us hope it will end up."

Clair looked back where the boy was picking up
the crying baby. He tried to shush it.
He had set down a big box of candy.   130

"Troy, I'm sorry," Clair said. "I can't help you."

Outside, the door opened onto a fire
escape. Clair climbed down one rickety set
of rungs to the next landing, which in turn
had lost its ladder. Below, thirty feet
or so—and then the ground. Only a leap
away, though, stretched the next roof. A dormer
window was within grasp from the near edge
in case Clair made the leap but slipped her feet
on wet, black shingles. Rain tinked on her cape.   140

Gutsy, she made the leap across the gap
from fire-escape landing to the far roof
and sailed over certain, terrible hurt.
Her arms stretched out to clasp the dormer peak.
Dimly, she could see in the round window
an attic space inhabited by old
furniture. The bottom pane was unlatched.

Within, a small lamp on a bedside night-
stand barely illumined the inhabitant.
There sat an ancient man, gaunt, white bearded,   150
in blue pajamas, eyes fixed on Clair's cape,

blissful eyes. "Holy Spirit, you have come,"
the man said, his breath piping a high note
behind his voice like a recorder flute.
"The angel is not as fell as I feared.
Surely, the Lord is in this place, and I
did not know it. How awesome is this day.
This is none other than the house of God,
the gate of heaven." The room was narrow,
long, and still as a church empty at night.   *160*

Clair felt her own voice was an intrusion.

"No, sir, my name is Clair, and I will leave
you. I had no other way to escape
the theater. I snuck in your window
avoiding a terrible fall out there.
Someone has to get help for the baby."

The old man said, "You have done me no wrong,
for if you are led by the Spirit, you
are not under the Law. *You* are Spirit
personified. O great is thy glory."   *170*

The man then closed his lids. The musical
tones beneath his breath ceased. Clair stood awhile
before she went downstairs, found the passage through
the parlors where the man lived by himself.

She ran with utmost haste in her bright foil
and reported to the witches what she'd
encountered.

Donning black raincoats with hoods,
they speed-walked through the wet night—*so slowly*,
thought Clair. When they arrived at the movie
house, they had missed the dancers who perhaps   *180*
had gone in time to climb their own windows
before their parents woke and saw them gone.

The boy had fled, leaving the baby and
young mother still upstairs, sobered somewhat
to see a horde of ladies dressed in black.
The girl muttered that her parents disowned
her for her pregnancy and had nowhere
to go. Mrs. Smith offered them shelter,
for her and the baby, with families
friendly to the Ladies' Society.   *190*

Almost forgetting the old man next door,
Clair showed them where he lay in his silence.
The house suggested he was a hermit:
a Bible, teapot, and, framed on one wall,
a painting of brown weeds were all he owned
beside three drawers with jeans and flannel shirts.

Smith paid two neighborhood men to construct
a wooden casket. "What shall we have them
inscribe on the top, Clair?"

                              Exhausted, she
spat out the first line that came to her head: *200*
"Lived faithful, forever, in the Spirit."

Four mornings later, in abiding sun,
Clair flew before her early writing time
to see the pine box set into the soil.

Chapter 20

Lovers at the Waterfall

Armed with a staple gun and a backpack
filled with rolled posters, Clair ran the Cities
and stopped at street-corner telephone poles.
The posters advertised a big meeting:

> **DISCUSS THE FUTURE
> OF OUR COMMUNITY
> BAND TOGETHER—
> SAFETY, CIVILITY
> MUTUAL WELL-BEING
> FRIDAY @ 7 PM
> MINNEAPOLIS INSTITUTE
> OF THE ARTS THEATER**

The day was an August Great-Plains scorcher,
the sky smogged up with smoke from far-off fires.
Clair's mission of the day felt tedious
and directionless, but as she wound south
block by block she realized the flipside
of not having to visit the Hmong Clans   10

or Somali City again today
was she basically could follow her whim.
By now her body had grown accustomed
to a slow marathon every afternoon.
Proud, she knew she was ten—a hundred!—times
tougher now than the cross-country runner
she'd been before. She'd soar past Janet Chang
from East Wayzata if they faced again.
But she supposed her racing days were done.

Free, she followed blocks south like a staircase   20
and arrived at Minnehaha Falls Park,
derived like so many Minnesota
place names from Longfellow's Indian poem.
Clair knew she could fill her bottles up here.
Like at every park, people grew gardens
and in between plots, prairie grasses stood
in horsetails, yarrow feathers, blue fescue.
Families with children and lovers still
leaned over limestone, waist-high walls and looked
at Minnehaha Creek's frothy free-fall   30
to the basin bed where she snaked away
in the final stretch as herself before
exchanging her last name "Creek" for "River."
Clair'd always liked the old sentimental
trope that bodies of water were female.
She let herself stand, rest, and drink water
from one of the fountains, definitely
not the creek which had fecal coliform.

Part of her wanted to troop down the steps,
immerse herself in one of the oxbows   40
like she used to do when she was little,
making her parents wait for hours as
she picked in the clear pools for stones, tadpoles,
minnows when there was all the time of youth.
But Clair wasn't too good at relaxing
anymore. So she turned from the falls and
memory. The past only brought sadness.

A rare sight: a man in a fancy suit
arm-in-arm, tight against a thin woman
in a black designer dress strolled ahead,   50
blind to the world in a cloud of romance.
The garden-dirtied city dwellers saw
the pair and stared as though at a slick ad
for a luxury hotel in Bali
they'd never get to visit in their lives.

Clair recoiled in recognition of them.
Dawn's dad was arm-in-arm with Jessica.

Clair turned and went down the stairs to the stream,
racing below, trying not to slap her feet.
At the bottom of the stairs, near fall's foot,   60
she checked behind her. They were descending.
Clair crossed the stream bridge and hid behind it.

The pair, thinking nobody was watching,
stopped halfway down and embraced each other.

Jessica reached behind his head and pulled
down for a passionate, open-mouthed kiss.

Clair followed the stream and made her escape.
She ran to stay ahead on a straight route
along the creek then turned back through the park.

Gradually, she found the river road,   70
crossed the Franklin bridge, back to the tower.
Her backpack was still half full with posters.
Anna wasn't in their bedroom when Clair
came in and fell into her bed, sweaty.
How easily a room spins from the view-
point of one's bed. She needed to light fire
to her feelings until there was nothing
left but ashes in which she could find rest.
She had thought she would quit, but she couldn't.
Nothing could be done except run and run   80
some more and staple up the damned posters.

When the elevator stopped, Mrs. Jones
was operating the button panel.

"Up or down, dear?" she monotoned, patient.

"I have energy to burn and posters
to put up," Clair said.
                    "You mean to go down."

Clair thought for a minute.
                    Jones just stood there,

index finger pointed at the panel.

A courageous, experimental part
of Clair's mind wondered what would happen if   90
instead of running, she *stared* at the fear,
the problem she either witnessed or caused.

"Do you know, Mrs. Jones," she said at last,
"if Mrs. Smith is upstairs, presently?"

Jones said she was upstairs, corresponding.
Clair looked up from the button and toward Jones.

"Then please press UP. I have to speak with her."

Jones got off at the writing offices.
Clair kept going up to the topmost floor
where she'd first met Mrs. Smith.
                              But the prim
schoolmarm of a lady astonished Clair.   100
Quite in contrast to the leather sofas,
burnished cone-shaped lamps, and the grand fireplace,
Smith was wearing an old, worn, gray sweatshirt,
UNIVERSITY OF MINNESOTA
written in faded red and gold printing,
the sleeves pulled up to her elbows and jeans.

"Ah, Clair!" she cried. "Forgive me my grubbies."

Clair apologized three times, to which Smith
said she ought to stop apologizing.   110

"I'm sorry for being obsequious."
Mrs. Smith laughed. "So what seems to be wrong?"
Clair described what she had seen at the falls.

Smith's face grew very serious, as if
she were chewing the inside of her gums.
She sat down, as did Clair without asking.
Lion-like, Tug took the middle cushion.

"Do you know why Jessica was with him?"
Clair said, "I think it has to do with me."
"Your thinking is correct."
                              "That's terrible!"   120

For once, Smith looked genuinely chagrined.
"Your friend's father is a philanderer,
besides being a powerful fellow.
I told you our business is persuasion.
Unpleasant as it may seem to a girl,
a woman's greatest power to persuade
is to lure a man with what he wants most.
Almost all of the most powerful men
in our world are willing to throw it all
away for what any pretty girl has.   130
Why would we neglect our most potent strength?
Because it offends sensibilities?
Unlike the wars of men, nobody dies."

Clair's feeling flared. She pointed at the witch.
"But I wouldn't want *my* father tempted.

We easily could destroy families."

The cat jumped up into Mrs. Smith's lap.
"Correction. We're saving *your* family.
Jessica's sacrifice has bought your home."

"So you'd seduce Dawn's dad just to save my house?"   140
Clair heard her own stern tone and didn't care.

"Me? Haha. Not likely anymore. Clair.
He already had several mistresses
in Minneapolis, New York, Paris.
I told you we'd do everything we could
to help your family. Everything.
I wonder when you'll alter your pronouns."

"Pronouns? What do you mean?"
                              "You. I. We. Us."

Slow, Clair went over to the grand window
looking east. She could almost imagine,   150
beyond downtown, the bluff where the house stood.
Yes, she felt some satisfaction knowing
it was safe. She couldn't deny the fact,
however crummy, that she cared much more
for her own kin than for a former friend
who would live in a mansion anyhow.

"Does the house now officially belong
to my folks? Do they have to make payments?'

"It is intelligent of you to ask.
Yet we must wait for Jessica to tell   *160*
us more. In the meantime, another threat
is brewing, an invasion from the east."

Clair turned around. Mrs. Smith was standing.
Behind her a bookcase stood askew and
ajar, a secret door in the wall with
a portal on darkness.
                              "Where does that go?"
Clair asked.
                  "Stairs going down. Fire exit,
really," Smith said. "I like the bracing draft."

Clair returned to the invasion topic.
"From the east? Do you mean Europe? Asia?"   *170*

Smith waved an arm at the idea. "No, no.
The eastern suburbs. They want all the food
growing in your parents and neighbors' yards.
The flyers you posted today were meant
to gather allies to mount a defense.
The starving eastern suburbs will strike first,
and soon the other suburbs will follow."

Clair remembered the rude men at the gate
into Woodbury, how cocksure they'd been
of their might. "My house, saved for nothing, then?"   *180*

"I doubt it. We're not so bumbling as that.
But you can help by refilling your bag with
more posters from below. Go spread the word."

"I'm sorry, Mrs. Smith," Clair said, "I think."

One of Smith's Uni-balls was poised to write.
"I told you to stop apologizing."

Clair apologized again and went down.

Anna was hard at work in the printing
room, a little closet beside the writing
offices, lifting and cranking an old   190
hand press. Her cheeks were smudged with black ink and
the once-white apron she wore looked as if
she had been accosted by preschoolers.
Wordless, Clair squeezed in and started rolling
the posters her roommate labored over.

Chapter 21

Stop Signs

1

After each day's composition, Clair ran
until dinner, sometimes well into dark
on warm summer nights until she became
a well-recognized figure passing by.
The gardeners and merchants manning their booths
along the sides of Clair's most frequent paths
would see her and say, "Do you ever rest?"

Around a fountain at a city park
she saw ladies serve vanilla ice cream,
homemade with ice, rock salt, goat cream, sugar,   *10*
to bearded homeless men who easily
could've been forty-niners gold mining
to find just dust, madness, and at long last
pay dirt in a paper cup. How they grinned.

"Hey, Clair!" one called. "Rest awhile and have some!"
She gave her thanks and ran in place while one

of the ladies scooped her a cone, then ate
it on the fly.
        They cried, "So long, runner!"

2

One cool morning delivering a note
on a dirt trail torn up by BMX   20
bikes in a corner of Como Central
Park, Clair saw two snakes, one black, one garter,
a blob-like bullfrog she moved to the grass,
and calling out from the neck of a dead
tree, three owlets, fluffy, white, chicken-sized.
She stopped her run and saw them contemplate
the great first leap with plenty of nervous cheer.
In the same spot two weeks closer to fall,
the owlets were gone, but maybe still there,
bothered by a mob of crows arrived there,   30
cawing out those who'd threaten them at night.

3

One Friday morning, Jessica returned
from who-knows-where, enclosed in a black cloak.
Clair had just stepped out of the tower door.
Jessica was talking with Jeremy.
It was early enough that the streetlights
were still on. In an urgent but hushed voice,
the musician made pleas to her down-turned
face. They didn't seem to notice Clair there.

"*Please*, Jessica," Jeremy was urging.   40
Their daughters were home in bed, ignorant
of the complicated trade-offs adults
make. Clair ran away from them into dawn.
How almost-silent feet fall when they land
on the toes first, as if climbing a hill.

4

Two big, well-made Midwestern houses burned
together just off Selby Avenue.
Clair stopped to watch at night on her way "home."
Flowers hung down from window boxes like
they were calling for someone to save them.   50
But no fire trucks were fueled up to come.

Neighbors watched and wept. One man kept saying,
"I told him he couldn't bring his charcoal
grill into the kitchen. I told him not
to." With narrow urban yards, the first house
had lit the second house aflame, candles
held close to each other. Smoke poured through cracks
in the bubbling stucco walls, white and black,
until one roof caved, launching a gray cloud.

5

She saw boys wrestling for a bald hilltop,   60
one challenging the champion after
another tossed opponents into dirt
with leg takedowns, body locks, firemen's throws.
Obesity had no place on the crown
of the hill, no shame in shirtless grappling.
Clair couldn't tell whether they were grinning
when they tapped out, or grimaced in their pain,
nor what caused the unbidden thrill she felt—
desire or violence. When they saw her there,
she fled to greet North Minneapolis.   70

6

Clair detoured to Kenwood where a good school
friend lived in one of the grandest mansions
in Minneapolis. Clair slowed to view
the bountiful vegetable gardens where
once lawns had grown. No one answered the door,
but shouts echoed from beyond the back wall.
Sneaking, yes, sneaking over a locked gate,
through an arbored grapevine tunnel, Clair found
the Olympus of backyard pool parties.
She imagined herself shedding her vest   80
of water bottles, her sweat-stinking shirt,
her overworked running shoes to join them,
her friend and half the kids she knew from school,
in that great marble bath of enjoyment.

Yet Fate had banished her as an exile
from the immortal fun of teenagers.
Duty called: a satchel full of letters.

She vowed against more nostalgic detours.

7

A wicked bout of menstrual cramps struck her
for two days, and Mrs. Smith understood   90
a hiatus was in perfect order.
After four hours of composition work,
however, Clair's muscles twitched for movement.
In the park at the base of the tower
she caught wind of a piano playing,
followed that sonata-wind to its source,
and should have known it was Jeremy's house.

Clair tapped on the front door to preserve sound,
and one of the black-braided twins peered forth.
Inside, the girls were painting bumblebees.   100
The piano music ran through the house;
it seemed to resonate from the floorboards.
Jeremy sat, bent over his keyboard,
hypnotized by the spell of music.
Then Clair watched him stop, sit up from bending
over the keyboard to make musical
notations. Hence, he'd play and sway, glance out
the open doors to the hosta garden.

Clair recalled spying on her own father
laboring on his lines in his study   110
little differently than Jeremy now.

In one of those rare but certain hunches
intimating the future, Clair felt sure
she'd one day need her own creative work—
to construct something her own, not borrow,
buy, or simply to watch others create.
For now she would *do*, then *rest*, later *make*.

Jeremy stopped playing, spun on the bench,
and said, "I'm working on six masterworks
in six years' time. This is the last project,   120
and it's almost finished. But lunch comes first."

The five of them ate tomato and fresh
basil sandwiches with some English tea.
The company of the girls precluded
talk of Jessica, seduction, the deal
that sent Clair to the tower, or old gods.
The shaman was plain before his own girls.

All quiet, they ate, watched a hummingbird
hover between the heads of pink bee balms.
Clair hadn't felt her cramps through the whole hour.   130

"Ah! A lovely respite in Paradise,"
Jeremy declared. "Now it's back to work."

Chapter 22

The Twin Cities Treaty

The week leading up to Friday's meeting
put enormous demands on Clair's two feet.
Besides stapling up scores more meeting posters,
she delivered messages between groups—
the East-side Hmong Clans, Somali City,
Dinkytown, Longfellow, Como, Seward,
the so-called Calhoun Beach Club, Prospect Park,
Frogtown, and North Minneapolis, too.

These groups hadn't rubbed shoulders together
since the city schools shut down, and they weren't
exactly friends then. Clair didn't see how   10
they were going to get over to East
St. Paul, if that's where the invasion came,
from the starving suburbs of Woodbury.

The leaders had seen enough of her now,
so that they didn't have their people stash
their pistols, hunting rifles, and other guns
when she showed up at their meeting places,
empty schools, rec centers, and fresh-plowed fields.

Her zig-zags progressed across the metro
with one step, then another, and so on.   20
She told Anna she had to sleep that night,
no candle-burning chats, she was so tired.

It was something to see the tower girls
and women get dressed before the meeting
and sit together at dinner fluffed up,
if only because the routine was changed.

True to Clair's idea of them as witches,
they wore mostly black: Mrs. Smith and Jones
in their best old schoolmarm uniforms and
Jessica ready for New York nightlife,   30
Anna in a knee-low dress suitable
for a funeral, others much the same.

Clair was stuck with a hand-me-down Easter
dress from one of the other girls, pink frills
and fake flowers crowded on far too much
fabric to suit Clair's lean, athletic frame.
At dinner she felt like a flamingo
misplaced among ravens.
                          Excited talk
about the meeting and all that was done
to bring together the Cities' powers   40
only added more juice to the fat steaks
they ate with mashed red-B potatoes, green
beans, and cherry pie. Clair had eaten more
meat in her three months than camel herders

in the Sahara ate in a full year,
she was sure of it.

        "Did you put posters
along Central Avenue?" one girl asked.

"Yes, Paige," Clair said. "And also Hennepin
and Broadway. My feet bear the blistered proof."

Jones broke in, "I predict a good turnout."   50

"Not a *noteworthy* one? Or *prodigious*?
Don't we have better synonyms than *good*?"
asked Anna, who was feeling grandiose
and was getting back at the Editor.

Jones replied, "I avoid hyperbole."

A bus arrived on University,
chartered, no doubt, at enormous expense.
The eight Society ladies who lived
in the witch's hat tower loaded up
together but disembarked at separate   60
stops approaching the Institute of Arts
to avoid the appearance of coming
together as a suspicious coven.

Not without teasing, Anna had to leave
the bus first, five blocks from the museum,
whereas Clair got off at the park in front
of the marble steps and guarding lion

statues. There had always been sad, homeless
men in the park whenever she'd been there
with her art-fiend parents or on school trips,   70
but now the hilly land was filled with tents,
not big green army tents but camping tents,
and she saw families in large numbers.

Some of the homeless were shuffling up
to see what the big meeting was about.
As far as Clair could see in the foyer,
the statues and paintings were all still here
tended by volunteers with name stickers.
The amphitheater was packed, standing
room only. Every corner and ethnic   80
group in the Cities was represented.

The Gardeners sat or stopped away from each
other with Mrs. Smith before the stage.

Not long after Touger Lor, leader of
the East-side Hmong clans began with, "Welcome,"
the meeting devolved into arguments.
They argued over who should be in charge
of which neighborhoods, though the divisions
were obvious to anyone who knew
the streets—especially to one who ran   90
them, daily—without ever approaching
the core issue, suburban incursions.

Mrs. Smith rose at one point and spoke up.
"All of your turf fighting will be for naught

if we don't agree upon a defense pact,
a treaty to stand up for our neighbors."

The Tent Folk, dressed in brown coats and knit caps,
with long-unwashed faces said, bitterly,
"We have nothing to lose. What can they take?
Oak trees that we call roofs? Street gutters we   100
relieve ourselves in? Our fires? Acorn gruel?
So, no. Invasions won't frighten us much.
Outside this grand museum, you can walk
from makeshift tent to tent and find civil
society. We read poems out loud,
debate a better form of government,
strum guitars to soothe babies and pass time,
invent economic systems around
barter. Despair, the banks, and joblessness
first brought us to the parks. And we'd perhaps   110
prefer to live in warm apartments, homes,
but we have never known so many friends
as we do here. Invaders will skip us,
for they will find nothing valuable
to take from our tents. Invisible is
our wealth beneath the trees. Food is what we
need, *not* security. Let's discuss food!"
They turned away. Without chairs, they huddled
together, standing in the back corner.

Clair threaded through bodies to find the ear   120
of John Stilgoe, agreed-upon Tent Folk
spokesperson, and whispered so he could hear,
"This alliance, John, may strengthen the bonds

between all groups today. East-side Hmong clans
can grow food for everyone, Tent Folk, too.
You, meanwhile, have governance expertise,
methods for democratic, equal, fair
decisions. We all need your leadership."

John pushed a streak of dirt around his face.
"I don't know who you are, girl. However,   130
I like what you have to say. Now let me
confer with my grove brothers and sisters."
She left, and they all seemed to speak loudly
at once.

       Far in front of the theater,
the Somali City people who live
in high-rise buildings along the river
were holding forth: "Let us speak   listen please!
We learned hard   how to fight   in our land   awful strife
with warlords   Al Shabaab militias   the British.
Yes, we'll fight   if need be   but don't think   we desire   140
more bloodshed.   You don't know   our culture   the beauty
we protect.   You're all drab   in our eyes   nothing bright
as our blues   pink and gold   our Koran.   Don't think we're
your army.   Rather, please   come to see   our culture
as treasure   from afar.   Our children   however
do require   medical care   in exchange.   For this boon,
certainly   we would fight   to protect   our neighbors."

Before speaking to Somali City,
Clair visited Y'Vonne Johnson within
the North Minneapolis caucus. She   150

was chief physician at a large clinic
up on Broadway for children and women.
She'd given Clair a shot for tetanus
after the girl had cut her arm on barbed,
rusty wire delivering a missive.
Y'Vonne remembered Clair and heard her out.

"Doctor, won't you please treat the Somali
kids? They clearly require your clinic's
good care. Meeting their needs could bring a peace!"

Dr. Johnson said, "You do get around,   160
don't you, Clair? We like joking that the sound
of feet on pavement will bring your behind
and news that's seldom good. But I don't mind.
Some say the Somalis don't respect us,
as if we're not African enough. Thus,
our relationship isn't quite what I
would hope. Yet it's convenient for white
residents around here to pit the two
African groups against another so
a powerful new black majority   170
can't shake the status quo in this city.
Nevertheless, it's time we reconcile
as neighbors. And you should know, all this while,
the clinic has been giving free healthcare
to all women and children who come there
though we may have to send them out to get
their pills or devices from the market."

Clair thanked and thanked Dr. Johnson and ran
to tell the Somalis about the news.

Touger Lor spoke on behalf of East-side   180
Hmong Clans, the indigenous people who
traveled to Minnesota after they
had helped America in Vietnam
and for their efforts were exiled from Laos.
Touger always received Clair's messages
nicely, whether she found him in a field
where old women and men planted veggies,
or at a rec center near Phalen Ave.
Dynamic, he was not only a voice
for the Hmong but a performance artist.   190

"Hey! You people! I'm the Hmong dude
from the State Fair! That dude wearing
break-dance clothes and this big-ass blue
belt you see here, right? But I'm not
here to make fun of those white school
teachers who thought Hmong kids can't get
English, and so they give A's for
writing, like, two right paragraphs
even while we make whole books of
poems about hot girls, wheel rims,   200
shooting deer for dinner, *real stuff*.
We got loads to offer city
people. We know how to fight, and
elders teach us how to grow food—
green peas, lettuce, sweet potatoes.

We want help with digging, planting,
and harvesting. My back aches, just
thinking about field work. Okay?"

Clair still stood near the Somali City
area listening to Touger Lor.   210
First, before she talked to him, she fought through
adults who clogged the aisles until she reached
the old lady who led the Calhoun Beach
Club and who listened to Clair, nodding her
head, finally.

       A white man in black clothes
had grabbed the mic to declare, "Blasphemers,
repent your sins! The end is surely near!"

The meeting suddenly seemed to lose steam.
Some parents who had brought their kids began
to get up to avoid the brimstone speech.   220
They were making Clair's once-hummingbird speed
to reach the East-side Clans impossible.

Mrs. Smith saw the problem and thought fast.
With gnarled hands, she wrestled the man in black
to steal the mic away from his doomsday
rhetoric. Clair had barely moved two rows.
Babies were crying. Groups were dispersing.

But then, Mrs. Smith wrenched the mic away.
At first, she seemed to be without a plan
but began to sing in her wobbly voice: 230

All who love and serve your city, all who
bear its daily stress, all who cry for peace
and justice, all who curse and all who bless,
in your day of loss and sorrow, in your
day of helpless strife, honor, peace, and love...

Moved by the lyrics, or just stricken still,
audience members froze where they stood, so
that Clair could take the opportunity
and weave once more, a pink hummingbird who
could fly through a prairie. Before Smith reached   240
verse two, Clair had made way to Touger Lor.

She cried, "The Calhoun Beach Club has machines—
rototillers, tractors, a plow that you
can use! Touger, will the Hmong sign a pact
uniting the Cities, once and for all?
Listen, don't forget the intelligence
I brought you. Your people in East St. Paul
will be hit first. You *need* the others' help."

Nodding his head, the Hmong leader was sure
of the truths this running girl had brought him   250
though he had no idea where she received
her information from.

                    Clair continued,
from one leader to the next, whispering
reminders of each one's local concerns.
With an echo effect, each spoke in turn

about the need for safety and secure
boundaries which could best be protected
with a mutual security pact.
The groups, from every ethnicity and
neighborhood, rose in waves of agreement.   260

Clair stepped aside from the departing mob
into the foyer. Down the hall hung Chinese
tapestries of serene peaks where sages
were content to sit alone there dwarfed by
Nature's awe.

On the bus ride back, quiet
ruled the ladies, the hour being past midnight—
well past. Clair sat sideways with her legs straight
in the aisle.

One ahead, Mrs. Jones turned
to speak, Clair guessed, for her unlady-like
deportment. "What you did was masterful,"   270
Jones said, instead. "When factionalism
breaks out, one must persuade in small huddles,
remind each leader of his own concerns
and constituencies, and only then
find some common ground. I heard Mrs. Smith
say as much to the other girls waiting
for the bus to arrive."

Clair never liked
compliments, but Mrs. Jones only gave
them for the educational value.

Clair sat at her bed before lying down,   280
proud that she had helped broker a new peace
in a moment's need. *I didn't flake out*
under pressure, she thought, tearing off whole,
black toenails deformed from marathoning.

Chapter 23

Invasion of the Gardens

History loves terrible ironies,
even on a scale as small as a town,
a family, a person flipped upside-
down. Who would have guessed the residents of
Woodbury would venture to East St. Paul
on purpose. All the chain stores were built in
Woodbury. But they came in their cars and
trucks and mini-vans bowling over stands
that families had built along the roads
armed with weapons protected by the law,   10
loaded up on zucchini, cucumbers,
homegrown corn, eggs, tomatoes, new baked bread.

Clair was dispatched to remind all parties
of their agreement to defend against
incursions. On hurried legs she achieved
the twelve short miles to her old neighborhood
in an hour and a half (a PR).
It was October; a cool wind followed
the roads; she wore a light, sporty jacket;
maples had turned red and the lightest green.   20

Clair met with Touger and his armed nephews
and paunchy older men on a bike path
in what was now appropriately named
Battle Creek Park, down the road from her house.

Touger explained, "Dude, they hold an ace card—
fueled trucks they can use for raids and
break-ins. They then escape."

                    At that moment,
men Clair knew from the Somali City
came down a side path in a great hurry.
Whereas the Hmong wore camos for hunting,   30
the Somalis were dressed in urban chic,
designer buttoned-down shirts and black jeans.
For a moment, Clair thought how weird this was—
her, involved with strategies for defense,
a little white girl in athletic shorts,
in council under the very oak trees
where she and her folks used to walk their dog
with men so far removed from her old life,
her prep-school world, its spelling bees and grades.

Loud, one of the Somalis repeated,   40
"They hold streets   along the high   river bluff.
They figure they   can make good   a fast escape
along Burns   to highways.   The bastards
think it will   be easy   to occupy
cul-de-sacs   with the bluffs   at their backs."

Touger set out a gas station street map
on the path and asked which streets they controlled.
The invaders held White Bear Avenue
up the hill to Clair's parents' back alley.

Touger explained, "Those dumb-ass invaders   50
went down dead-end streets and are trapped like deer.
We now got more firepower with you all here."

But one of the older Somali men said,
"Civilians   still in homes   will get hit
in our fire   if we charge   in blindly."

Clair recalled mountain bike trails on the bluff
behind the houses most locals didn't
bother to explore. Only kids hiked them,
because of the poison ivy and ticks.
She used to run the trails, stop on over-   60
looks, and watch the big train yard and river.
(Who knows? She probably had Lyme's disease.)

"I could sneak in and lead them out the back,"
Clair announced. "Please give me at least an hour."

She followed a trail down into a deep
valley toward the Mississippi River.
Tall white pines stood sentry on the bluff sides.
She passed the mouth of a large sandstone cave,
then she cut up the side of a steep slope,
rapid, tiny steps like a bike's granny   70

gear. Clair barely even breathed hard uphill.
She remembered a past run through here once
when she chanced upon a couple getting
frisky in nature's bed. She ran so fast,
so quietly, the two never looked up.

The trail now levelled out with a meadow
surrounded by a stand of thin birch trees.
Quickly, she had to leap! A half-consumed
deer carcass lay across the single track.
Clair nearly stepped inside the hole left by   80
some scavenger, probably coyotes,
which she knew lived here in the woods behind
the neighborhood houses. She kept onward.
There was the faintest trail, made by turkeys,
whose quills scraped lines in the sandy substrate
to back yards along White Bear Avenue.

Clair heard gunshots in the distance, motors
that revved, cries and the shouts of angry men.

She emerged from the woods in a garden
plot spoiled by tire tracks and ruthless   90
harvesting. Half-chopped lettuce heads lay with
decapitated carrot tops, slaughtered
corn stalks, watermelon vines hacked like necks.
Stern talk came from a nearby garden shed.
Clair crept across the muddy, rutted rows
to reach the partially open shed doors.
"Please, please, let my son go," a man's voice begged.

A furious woman's voice responded:
"Shut up! You drove through here planning to steal
the food I grew to feed my kids' hunger.   100
You reap what you sow, and you didn't sow
a single seed for yourselves. So you thought
you could fuel up and drive in here to get
whatever you want. But you didn't think
us poor city farmers would fight like hell
to defend what we've slaved to grow ourselves."

Clair could make out the woman's back but not
the faces of the males through the door crack.

The man cried, "Yes! You're right! You're right—the food
is yours. But understand. We are starving   110
in Woodbury. The shelves at Rainbow Foods
are bare. No trucks have gas to bring them goods.
Some of us still have jobs in the Cities,
downtown, where we can buy food from you all.
But I was the Woodbury High football
coach. I taught History. They cut my job.
Football is frivolous when you're hungry.
But coaching and teaching were the only
things I knew how to do. I lived for them."

Clair thought of her own dad and his lost job.   120

A younger man's voice started to speak. "Dad,
let's just—"
            The older voice spoke over him.

153

"Look, I couldn't tell you the first thing
about gardening, how to grow your food.
Put your pitchfork down. Hey, my name is Mike.
This is my son, Kyle. We're desperate for food.
But we're still people. We have friends nearby!
Maybe you know them, too? Kelly and Sam?
They live a block away. Really nice folks,
like you, I bet. Wait! What are you doing?"   *130*

The woman's voice said, "Mike, you should have asked
Sam and Kelly for some food instead of—"

Slowly, without a creak, Clair pulled the doors
apart. The widening light was startling
to the woman who wielded the pitchfork—
she whipped around and took a stab at Clair,
but she was bumped from behind by her two
captives, who shoved past Clair through the shed doors.
They sprinted out of sight.
                        The pitchfork missed
Clair's ear. Now the woman was pointing it   *140*
at her chest. "Who are you? What have you done?"

Clair put her hands out. "I'm a messenger.
Excuse me for interrupting, but there's
a back-up force about to infiltrate
these streets and return your land back to you.
But first you've got to follow me into
the bluffs. Then they will push out these raiders."

The woman was furious, blood-thirsty,
Clair figured. But she was wrong. The woman
mumbled, "What's the point? We've lost all the food.   *150*
They'll take off when they've gotten everything
and return in the next growing season."

"Oh, no," Clair countered. She tried to explain
that others from the Cities were nearby
and newly organized to protect them.

"Well, they're a little late," the woman sighed,
resigned. The pitchfork lowered from Clair's heart.
For once, Clair's powers of persuasion failed.

She snuck from house to house and found the same.
Neighbors had no hope, and they didn't want   *160*
to leave home under any circumstance.
It was dishonest, anyway, Clair thought
to try and convince people not to feel
what she'd been feeling all along, herself—
she only wanted her parents to stay.
A nearby deer path led to the bluff trails;
she took one around to the regional
park, crossed Upper Afton Road and returned
to Touger's position. Clair reported
her failure.

"That's okay," he responded.   *170*
"Hey, no worries! We Hmong on the
Mekong River picked off soldiers

like these dudes who believe they won."

Then Clair decided to go home, not to
the tower, but to the house where her folks
probably huddled, despondent with fear.

Running the bluff trail, she came out behind
the alley, where she was surprised to see
zero trucks or trailers or invaders.
She saw the garden beds were still unharmed.   *180*
The tomato plants were jungly, unplucked.
The jade plant, for that matter, was unmoved,
more colossal than ever, on the deck
table. She knocked on the door to avoid
frightening her parents by bursting in.

Chapter 24

The Daughter Returns

Clair's mother heard the knock and was afraid
to open. That morning she'd awakened
and gone outside to find, with real horror,
three hornworms had consumed the tomato
plants' leaves from the tops—down a foot in one night.
They were longer than a middle finger,
fatter, and green with spots of bright yellow.
When she saw them it occurred to her then
that she had indeed seen their future form,
a truly lovely hawkmoth, fly away   10
just before, as she had opened the front gate.

"Ah! A hawkmoth," she'd exclaimed, happily—
then the worm. The parents laid it, before.
She went inside to find the kitchen tongs,
for the mandibles on those bugs can bite!
Back outside, she was on such a mission
to remove them before they did more harm,
she didn't register the sounds of trucks,
lots of loud motor engines, since birds and
rare backyard parties had been the only   20

noteworthy neighborhood sounds for a year—
that and the Jeep which brought them the bank's threat.
The truck noises were coming from Highway
10-61. Mary said, "Get off there,
bug," when the screams and shots made her drop him.
The hawkworm fell into the brown compost.

Lines of trucks spun into the back alley,
most with armed men standing willy-nilly
in pick-up beds leaning over cab tops.
Mary saw the head of one snap back and   30
arc in a reverse somersault, landing
in the pick-up bed. Down the block of chain-
linked backyards, she could see a neighbor fire
from behind everyone's disused, dead cars.
More shooting, faster than Roman candle
sparking, then sporadic like popcorn pops
at the end of a microwave cycle.
Rather than face further salvos, the trucks
sped on through the alley, back to the road.
They didn't return to the highway, though,   40
but drilled deeper into the neighborhood.
In the distance: more shouts, engine revs, guns.

The neighbor, a convicted drug dealer,
waddled into his garage with a gun,
which she doubted had ever been legal—
but what did she know about firearms?

Hours later, she saw some of the same trucks
speed down the main road with full loads of produce.
Like a pirate with bottles of spiced rum,
one glutton held two heads of romaine up   50
before he bit off half of one and chewed.
Clair's dad peered out the windows, astonished,
but not as anxious as one might expect.
Perhaps he didn't worry what happened
here as much with Clair away, somewhere safe.
And with that thought, Clair appeared on the front
step. She knocked, and Mary opened the door.

Clair was changed. She looked older but also
tougher, wiry, a figure from outside
the American Age of Comfort and   60
Ease, a girl who belonged among Spartans,
or with Sioux Indians who would've travelled
without ceasing long between great hardships
of sun, heat, thirst, distances that we can't reckon.
Her own daughter looked harder than anyone
she'd grown up with or known but in pictures
from *National Geographic*.

                    "Hi, Mom,"
Clair said. "I'm glad to see that you've survived.
But what happened to the tomato plants?"

Chapter 25

Unrequited Desires

Clair felt she had what people call closure.
She reported to her parents the bank
was probably relinquishing its claim
on the house, but she forbade all questions.

Her parents didn't look like they believed
her.

    "It's true, Mom and Dad. We saved the house.
The wit—, er, *Mrs. Smith* pulled powerful
strings. She has connections I can't describe.
And the invaders soon will be vanquished."

She saw how her folks looked at her in awe,   *10*
as odd as that sounded. As if she'd come
back from the Navy SEALs but different—
neither her mom nor her dad made attempts
at turning back the clock, turning her back
to the fragile girl who had needed them.
No return to "Mommy missed you so much,"
though she would have accepted it with love.

No "we've kept your bedroom just as you left
it," nor "let me whip up your favorite mashed
potatoes with skins on and garlic." None.   20
No family sentimentality.

Mary did say, "Tell us about your...school."

Clair said she found the "Tower School" nice but
rigorous in some ways her old school could
not imagine, let alone advertise.

"Well, I love how your diction has improved,"
said Paul, Clair's dad. "Vocab is important."

They ate cucumber sandwiches and sweet
potato fries. "You don't have to worry
about me," Clair said, and left off hoping   30
that they would trust those words and her promise
to drop by whenever she could come near.

"Alexander the Great ruled half the world
at scarcely a younger age," she heard Dad
say to Mom when she went to the bathroom.
(Ah! a toilet! how often she'd squatted
or just held it on her messenger runs!)
In the bedroom where nobody lived now,
she dug in her dresser for underthings,
two more pairs of running shorts, some school clothes   40
for her writing lessons and rare downtimes
in the tower, as well as some hair bands—
they bulged in the pouch of her running vest.

She headed back toward the tower via
downtown St. Paul, a ghost town in the best
of times but curiously vacant now.
She presumed news of the invaders spread.
Nevertheless, she enjoyed frolicking
over the fake boulders by the fake creek
in Mears Park even while seeing many   50
stores and restaurants closed made her feel sad
for all the people who'd lost their incomes.
They couldn't manipulate the bankers
like the Gardening Society did.

Then she came to Rice Park where the X-mas
lights had never been taken down last year.
She decided the Landmark Center still
looked stately though she could not pretend that
it was a castle like she used to do.

Grander, though, was the fact the Central Branch   60
Library still opened its innocent doors.
The librarians were said to come each day
to lend and protect the books without pay.
That's what she should have done, Clair decided,
if she hadn't become the messenger
and a rhetorical witch-in-training.

Clair resisted the urge to enter and
spend the entire day combing through the stacks
for those obscure titles only Central
Branch might possess somewhere on the third floor   70

or in the basement available by
passing a slip to the librarian.
Oh the lives and the books (one and the same)
we will never have time to make love to!

Clair couldn't believe she just had that thought.
She promised to take the next quiet day
and run here with nothing to do but read.

But with the invasion, there was no time.

She needed to report to the tower.
She said good-bye to the marble façade,   80
its sheer pink expanse, the fine cornice work.
Uphill past the Romanesque cathedral,
the High Bridge out of sight to the far left,
a quick recovery down flat Selby
Ave., brownstones and big Midwestern houses,
north to University Avenue,
trash strewn (Styrofoam and plastic wrappers
survive forever), empty used car lots,
vacant big boxes, but the sky was wide.
White clouds were combed in one long ponytail.   90

Chapter 26

The Two Blades

And suddenly, up University,
foot traffic came in a crowd, parents with kids,
men pushing strollers and handcarts with food,
caravans of bicycles in tandem.
Finding a pace was impossible with
the weaving.

      "What is everyone fleeing
from?" Clair asked a woman slow-winged with kids.

"An attack," she said. "Men with cars and guns."

Clair protested. "You're going the wrong way.
They came from Woodbury to East St. Paul."   *10*

"No, no. They're behind us, across the bridge.
They swarmed Minneapolis from the west."

Clair thanked the lady and doubled her pace.

Two invasions? The city was sandwiched.
Farther down, University clogged up
with more residents-become-refugees.
None knew where to go, having left their homes.

Clair thought she saw the back of Dawn's mom's head
but it didn't turn to Clair's calls—then, saw
Dawn with her, frantic, carrying a knife.   20
Clair could not reach her but called out Dawn's name.
She pushed to get within range of hearing.

"What are you doing here?"
                          Could make out bits:
"—Dad left us—stayed with my aunt—men with fire—"
Dawn clenched the knife as she yelled. Clair knew it,
Grandpa Leigh's fishing knife, left at Dawn's house.

The river of the crowd took them away.
What a throng: families with full strollers,
boys and girls wearing quick-stuffed school backpacks,
long-unused cars puttering or slow-pushed,   30
everyone mirroring a state Clair knew
from experience—Panic, the goat god
appearing for the first time in their lives,
many of them, eyes expanding as black holes.
For they saw their comfortable, safe islands
had been situated in the wild sea.
Clair was alarmed but free from panic's grip,
as though the poison had made her immune,
or she had found some cure in a virus.
She dodged and shoved her way against the stream   40

toward a growing thunderhead of black smoke.

Prospect Park, the neighborhood surrounding
the witch's hat tower, was not in flames,
not the homes, but rather the grand old oaks.

Men doused the tree trunks in gasoline—gas!—
and ignited them with long grill lighters.
Near the hill around the tower's wide base,
salvos of gunfire went back and forth, which
Clair knew she was crazy to approach but
she did anyway. Embers fell from leaves,   50
bright snow that burned. The air was mostly smoke.
The heat made Clair feel like she had landed
on a planet much closer to the Sun,
unsuitable for life and human beings.

A terrific roar of shouting sounded.
"Go back to where you came from, you damn pigs!"
Jeremy, in an unseasonal coat,
laughed, firing his AK-47
at men hiding behind the tower's edge.

The musician was shielded in fierce flames.   60
The men, popping pistols, couldn't reply
adequately to Jeremy's fury.

Clair wanted to ask him where his daughters
were hiding or gone to, but there was no
getting closer. Then glass crashed on the flag-
stones. Clair looked up. The barrel of a gun

pointed out of one of the high windows.

Jeremy didn't see where the shot came
from, but he fell back against the last trunk
unburnt in the park. The men, now brave, charged,   70
fired loud shot after shot into the punk
rocker's woolen overcoat. Still, he fired
back in spite of his wounds and made them duck.

Finally, he fell and Clair ran to him.
She couldn't see any bloody bullet
holes in his chest. He lay back, grinning wide.

"Listen, Clair," he said. "Kin die. Cattle die.
What never dies is the glorious dead!
Hahahahahahahahahaha!"
Then Jeremy, still smiling, closed his eyes.   80

Clair heard gunfire whiz by. The men approached.
She hurried around the back of the tower
to the unguarded door.

                    Quiet and cool,
the inside seemed as if it were immune
to strife. The elevator responded
to the bell and button for the top floor.

When Clair was nine, and Paul Wellstone had died
in the plane crash a week before voters
could re-elect him, her parents had wept.
Her father called it a conspiracy.   90

Clair paced around the house, avoiding them,
unsure of how to act or what to say.
Nobody said anything at dinner.

Now Clair wanted to kick the ironwork
sides of the elevator and vomit,
for Jeremy, one of her friends, was dead.

The elevator hummed up, bumped a little
at the top, and Clair opened the steel gates.
The far window was broken, roughly.
There was no Smith or Jones or Jessica   100
to explain. Instead, armed with a rifle
practically equipped with a telescope,
sitting back-straight in Mrs. Smith's armchair,
was Nat.

        "What the hell are you doing here,
Nat?" Clair said, swearing in spite of herself.

"I told you land was the commodity
of the past—and the future. Here I am.
And I do like a nice tower, you know.
Now I have two of them. *The Two Towers!*
At least you might get my Tolkien jokes, Clair.   110
Unlike the men I have working for me."

To the left, she glimpsed the secret bookcase
unlatched and just open. Smith had escaped,
perhaps.

"As I ran here, I passed thousands
fleeing their homes, fleeing the savagery
you brought here from the past. Aren't you ashamed?
Don't you see, Nat, this isn't a daydream?
You're ruining the lives of human beings."

"I've ordered my men merely to fight those
who resist."

"They're families defending their homes!"   120

Nat shrugged. "Fire is needed to grow forests,"
he said. "And if time isn't cyclical,
why are the two of us in a tower,
and not for the first time? I mean it, Clair."

She took a gradual step toward the books
and said, "Why did you come to *this* tower?"

"Ah!" he replied. "Don't you recall the note
I sent with you? I know what they do here.
Seduction—and later, betrayal. I know.
These witches wrench apart families, too.   130
Do you know, Clair—did you know my parents
split up when we were in the sixth grade? Just when
my little *episodes* were beginning."
He sat on one of the leather sofas.
"You all do have fine taste, though, I must say."

169

Clair took note of the "you all"—and two steps
closer to him, but also to the door.

Nat's eyesight turned distant with memories.
"I'd never had one of those fits until
a night after I had turned eleven.   140
For my birthday my parents had bought me
a sword. A genuine broadsword they sell
in that weird knife store at the MOA.
You know, on the third floor, by that cool jet
simulator and Tony Roma's Ribs?
They would get me whatever I wanted,
and I wanted a real freaking broadsword!"
He chortled, and Clair smiled along, feigning.
"It was pretty sharp, and the point could kill
someone, definitely. That's love, I guess.   150
Anyway, one night not too long after,
I was staying up late watching TV.
My mom was away at a conference
for tax attorneys, so I could stay up
late as I wanted."

                    Outside, a loud boom
sounded. Nat moved to look out the window.
"It was just a big tree falling in flames.
Anyway, I was staying up watching
Letterman or inappropriate shows
on late-night cable when I got hungry.   160
I went downstairs to the kitchen"—his hand
followed the pathway he saw in the air—

"to find some leftover sausage pizza.
And that, Clair, was when I heard whispering."

She realized now he had told this story
to himself many, many times before.
Her feet were only a leap away from
the secret door, but she stayed to listen.
How had all this happened, and could she use
the information she learned against him?   170

"A forest fire isn't much to see
from above," he went on from the window.
"All smoke, few flames, not like *Bambi* at all.
The whispering came from the living room.
I entered the doorway, nonchalantly,
at first, pizza held to my face. And then
I went back to my room to get my sword.
I approached behind them, ready to strike.
Really, I was! Can you believe it, Clair?"
He turned to face her. "I almost killed Dad!   180
And the woman he was cavorting with.
Well, he saw me, and I could not do it.
That's when I had a total fit. Breakdown.
Somehow he led me back to my bedroom.
And he was really gentle. He stayed with me,
stroking my hair as we watched Letterman..."
He trailed off and was quiet for a while.
Another tree fell.

                    "I'm really sorry,"
Clair said. "I think things get complicated—"

"Yes, you should know how complicated, Clair.   *190*
Once I left school, I had time on my hands,
and the Internet. I did some research,
first on the woman who seduced my dad.
She was trying to convince him to quit
his refining and selling gas, you know.
She wasn't entirely successful,
but in a weird way she helped me get here.
I gave up on the late-night TV and searched
instead for this witch, Jessica Conrad.
Her name popped up all over Web archives,   *200*
not lately, but around ten years ago
she wrote letters to the editors of
newspapers and magazines, lots of them.
They were written with a certain formal,
almost archaic style. Nauseating
in their moralistic declarations.
Going even deeper, I found her name
in archived correspondence to Clinton
and Bush. But below her name in a few,
Highland Ladies Garden Society,   *210*
which then became the subject of my search.
They'd written hundreds, thousands of letters
going back a hundred years to the start
of Minnesota's statehood. Furthermore,"—
his voice lost the mild tenderness from when
he was talking about his father and
now he was making the senior-year speech
he'd never get to give—"societies
of these so-called ladies turned out to be

ubiquitous. They're all around the world,   220
and they've been steering men for centuries.
I cannot abide their hypocrisy,
made even worse by their moral preaching.
Do you deny any of this?"
                              "I don't."

He pointed his finger at her. "Do you
admit that men and their admittedly
carnal natures are manipulated?"

Clair knew she could spin a big, fat story,
work him into a knot, but she didn't.
She thought of Jessica and Dawn's father.   230
"Yes, it does happen. I am sorry, Nat."

He triumphed out loud. "That's why I sent you
here with that note! I knew they would take you.
How could they resist a young specimen
as intelligent as you—and pretty.
I always thought you were the prettiest
though I never guessed they would toughen you
up as they have. You're not a girl at all.
You're like the mom on *Terminator II*.
In fact, you could probably kick my ass.   240
Instead," he approached her, still with the gun,
"I thought you would kiss it. I'll make a deal.
Do what your kind does—prostitute yourself.
I will withdraw all my men across the bridge,
never coming close to your parents' house.
They'll be left in peace. Your dad was always

kind to me, and I wish him all the best.
You can still live in a tower—with me."

"Nat, I can't believe you said 'prostitute.'
You have no idea how to talk to girls."   250

He opened his arms, the gun in one hand.
"But you're a Society lady now.
And you're being offered a power deal."

Clair tried to imagine how the future
might be saved for her parents, for their house,
and for the families running in fear.
She had already saved the old house once.
Jessica had made the same sacrifice.
And now she would have to make it again.
How many sacrifices would be made?   260
The tower tipped and wobbled like a top
whose spin was losing its integrity.
Clair was still capable of vertigo.

Yet Nat didn't feel it. He smoldered on,
coming closer to achieve her embrace.

The future and the past, their conceptions,
were what sent Clair spinning. She could see this
truth, clearly, and the boy before her, whom
she knew in this moment she did not want.

"You don't know me, Nat, like you think you do,"   270
she said, backing toward the books. "And you won't."

He started to go wild when Clair dashed out,
downstairs, short quick strides, three steps at a time.
She kept tight against the bend, descending,
hidden from any shot on the spiral
stairs. She moved so fast he couldn't keep up,
nor the past, nor the future. Only *run*
in downward spirals, descending circles.

Chapter 27

Descent

Clair ran down the stairs, and they seemed endless.
Scant light from the bookcase door, open wide,
could not reach two turns of the spiral stairs,
so Clair stepped under the hope the next steps
down were as wide and as deep as the last.
Her left arm guided her along the wall.
The speed she went was faster than was safe.
Her nervous breathing came and went in gasps.

Behind and above, she could hear Nat's pace,
more uncertain and clodding with missteps.   10
A gun shot thundered in the staircase,
a momentary flash before the sound,
so loud and concussive with its echo,
as if a trash can had been thrown down from
the upstairs railing of a shopping mall.
Both Clair and Nat cried out. Her ears felt pain—
she heard as if she were underwater.

Then her hand, grazing along the stone wall,
felt not stone but rock, rough, craggy, cratered

with crumbly mortar, and she had to slow   20
as the steps turned more uneven, unknown.
She realized her backpack, stuffed with clothes,
slowed her down, so she slipped free and went on.
Above came a crash, a cat's cry, swear words,
and another shot. Then, a scream, silence,
before Clair could hear the start of moaning.
She continued her perilous descent
until she stumbled for lack of a step.
The stony floor leveled, and the rock wall
straightened out beneath her hand's grazing touch.   30
Above, the weeping—and a tumbling fall.

Out of nowhere, a memory came forth:
The spelling bee of Clair's seventh-grade year,
only her and Nat sitting on the stage,
the final contestants after ten rounds,
over an hour. The middle-school children
had been getting restless from sitting down
so long. Mr. Carlson, the principal,
had to get up to calm everyone down.

"Okay, boys and girls, I appreciate   40
you've sat here patiently this long. Thank you,
but Clair and Nat sure deserve our respect.
Let's face it: School isn't Utopia,
and we all have to—"
              While Carlson went on,
Clair turned to Nat and whispered, "Well, why not?"

Nat, who'd spent the contest staring into
the left spotlight, even as he spelled, said,
"What? Why not what?" He seemed not to see her
in the comparative darkness.
                She said,
"Why can't all of this be Utopia?"   50
Carlson had finished administering
his sedation. The auditorium
was near silent. Nat didn't turn around.

"You're right," he answered. "There's no reason why
it can't." The next word was ENTELECHY.
Nat went on to win.

             The memory made Clair
stop her flight, to turn and find her old friend.
I don't want to be a trickster, she thought.
With uncertainty, she turned and called out
his name. She felt her way upward and in,   60
then nearly fell over his fallen frame.

In the darkness, his voice: "I shot myself!
I fired, and the bullet ricocheted back.
I'm sorry. I just wanted to scare you."

And Clair, not trusting him but something else,
said, "We can't go back there. The passage leads
out just a bit up ahead. Come with me."
She tried to hoist him up, but the gun came
between them. "I can't carry you unless

you leave this stupid rifle behind us." 70
She noticed how loudly they were talking.

Nat replied weakly with a Midwestern
accent his confidence had covered up,
"I could, ah, use it as a walking stick."

Clair asked him where his injury was, and
he said his side. She thought of the English
class they shared in eighth grade, watching the film
versions of *Romeo and Juliet*.
In both, Mercutio was so surprised
to see the sword wound inflicting his side. 80

As if her thought had prompted his own, Nat
said, "'Tis not so wide as a church door, but
twill serve. Ask for me tomorrow and you—"

Clair finished for him, "—shall find me a grave
man."

He laughed between his groans and wheezing.
His grasp loosened on the neck of the gun,
or perhaps his strength was leaking out, red,
and Clair indeed felt she was stronger.
Thus, she could hoist him up and half-carry
his weight, shuffling, into the straight tunnel, 90
the gun dragging more than serving as cane.
He refused to leave it behind himself.
Clair could feel a wet spot near his hip bone.
Was that a faint light showing up ahead?

"You know," Nat started up, "that scientists
have found information can be sent non-
locally. I'm talking quantum physics
here. Bear with me since I know you doodled
through Science."

        All of Clair's stress coalesced
as though a line of white cumulus clouds   *100*
piled up, turned dark, and rained. So she threw up.

"You see, they shoot two particles away,"
Nat continued, "in different directions.
Then they get one to vibrate or something
sexy. Incredibly, its particle
friend, shot at the speed of light the other
way, begins to vibrate, *non*-locally."

The light was getting brighter and brighter.

"Who is to say then, Clair, that two persons
could not vibrate across great distances   *110*
in correspondence. Haha!" His weight grew
heavy. "Or, for that matter, across time.
I feel that I received a beckoning
from the past, as if I did not belong
or originate in this time. They speak
to me now, the voices of non-local,
long-dead lords, whom I sought to emulate.
They say—"

And there Clair saw where the witches
had gone. A great cavern, wider than tall,
without those stalactites or stalagmites   120
one would expect; it was filled with bookshelves,
rows and rows, a library archive like
Clair had always imagined was under-
neath the New York City library or
the Library of Congress in D.C.
Farther down the row of shelves, Anna came
pushing a cart stacked high with paper reams.
No doubt they were letters to be archived.

"So that's where they went," Nat said, changing his tone.
He tried to lift his walking stick, the gun,   130
so Clair squared toward him, pulling her support
from under his arm. He fell with a crash,
but no shot this time. In the light she saw
his blood-wet side as well as her own stain.
Farther, Anna had disappeared, cart-less.

Soon, the tower witches were surrounding
the two of them, appearing from the stacks.
Among them was Jessica with her twin
daughters.

            Nat saw her and said, "Look at me,
yet another weak male who has fallen   140
prey to his foolish desire for love.
Woe unto me, for I fell into the web."

Smith and Jones were here, the others, as well
as residents from the Prospect Park homes.
Tug was circling around Cassandra's legs.

Nobody lectured Nat, least of all Clair.
But they didn't call a doctor, either.

Chapter 28

Letter

To the parents of Nat Mortensen,

I dare not address this letter with *Dear Mr. and Mrs.*, though we personally met on a few occasions. How graciously you congratulated me for the writing prize and offered friendly consolation in my spelling bee losses to your now late son. Yet I fear you will not think dearly of me, considering the news and shock you certainly must feel finding this body curled on the bench at your door.

I sat beside Nat when he died. You deserve my best, most honest description of his final moments to remember him by.

I sat beside where Nat lay on a makeshift pallet in the dark chamber of a cavern. I do not know the degree to which you have been aware of your son's recent purpose. You must have seen enormous quantities of gasoline moved by his designs from your family's reserves. I leave it to you whether you wish to uncover his activities or leave them untouched to preserve his memory. Or perhaps you stood behind him these last months; I refrain from all moralizations, which he despised.

I only know that the boy beside me in that cavernous darkness was the same one I knew when we first met in sixth grade, a boy by turns awkward in his endearments—"O, clever Clair," or "Clair the Compassionate," he called me, though I deserve neither—but also a boy so marvelously confident in his literary erudition. At the end, he made allusions to Tolstoy's *The Death of Ivan Iliych*, which I have never read even while Nat continued to insist on a conspiracy of knowing (always his way).

"You'll recall the passage, of course," he said, "where Ivan, injured by his scarcely credible curtain-hanging mishap involving the idiotic upholsterer, finally approaches the Void after days of painful, mindless screams drove his family to tears. Light replaces pain; all of his greedy longing after imaginary, well-furnished rooms was forgiven; and the best line comes: 'Death is finished! It is no more!' Then he dies. Can you explain the paradox, O clever Clair? I think I can!"

Nat chatted as winsomely as he did in English 6, where I shall continue to remember him best. Not as he was on those days when he got back a test grade, which may have shown that he knew everything but the measly definitions he was supposed to study; rather, I remember him in the end as on those days when our hapless, well-intentioned instructor (my father) "opened the floor" for discussion on the previous night's reading. I see Nat sitting in the center of my classroom recollection, the 9:25 light of B period gleaming over the bookshelves, illuminating the tips of that unruly hair from behind. I can see every golden-edged strand and him holding forth just as he did for his final moments in the cavernous darkness.

Thus, I feel certain he knew the same transcendence Tolstoy had his character describe in violation of the miserable rules of Realism. One of my ears shall remain open for his holding forth. Like Tolstoy, Nat believed in the Beyond. Now he rests from all anxiety and knowledge, but what a boy should know of his own enthusiasms, including perhaps the fact that I am

The friend who came back for him,

Clair

The Walled Garden

Invaders don't stay long when they've raided
all that they can get, stolen food and goods,
and then, when the leader who first supplied
and commanded them exits the mayhem,
they scatter to the dictates of their greed.

Winter arrived. The witches and neighbors
who had returned after the invasion
mostly stayed below ground in the caverns
of canned goods and a well-stocked cheese pantry.
With fewer messages to deliver,   *10*
Clair explored lost tunnels leading into
the University rare book archives.
She wasted blissful hours falling in love
with the neglected volumes she found there.

Once, in a head-lamped reading reverie,
she thought she heard a whisper in her ear:
"You'll see. Nature, released by fire, made whole."
Clair thought, *So that's a synchronicity,*
and went back to reading John Milton's book.

At last, when spring thawed the earth and dropped rains,   20
we turned the city into a garden.
The ashes of invaders' fires made
good compost. Destroyed buildings and bridges,
and a few towers, went into the start
of the building of a great wall around
the Cities, its fruits and streams and people.

Clair ran the perimeter of the wall
while it was being constructed of stone,
reused rebar, hand-turned cement mortar.
She preferred running on grass, gravel, or dirt,   30
for she knew too much time on the asphalt
probably shortened a runner's career.
Clair could not believe how she used to let
herself become sick with anxiety.
So, more than before, she wasn't afraid
to halt her pace and observe a moment
as it moved outward. No competitor
nor fantasy horsemen of nervousness
threatened to catch up.

                  She stopped in a field,
a golden prairie meadow recently   40
plowed and reseeded from what was just weeds—
now purple hyssop, yarrow, and milkweed.
Nearby, growing in raised beds—hot peppers,
tomatoes, greens, and corn for the table.

She thought, *This is what we gardeners do.*
Her mother worked in her yard, and her dad
cultivated his own lines in his room,
as if no troubles had ever arrived
at their house, which now lay inside the wall.

Clair stood, admiring the reclaimed brownfield.   50
Someone had put up a house for bluebirds,
and a brilliant male perched on a fencepost
nearby. Unlike a blue jay, it was blue
in totality, bluer than the sky,
which for most people defines what blue is.
Then Clair saw a blander blue bird dart in
the opening to the house with some grub.
She smiled at the thought of babies nested there.

At that, a European sparrow flew,
dive bombing toward the house on its pole stand.   60
The male intercepted the sparrow and,
with a show of aerial wrestling,
sent the sparrow away. The female then flew off,
no doubt to find more food for the fledglings.

Clair wondered at the constant hurry, work,
and anxiety of the bluebird pair,
how they must find food and fret that when they
return from the fields, they will find their hopes
killed. And it happened every single spring.
Nor was it lost on her how the male helped.   70

Just as she started to take off, she saw
the sparrow return.

            "Shoo, shoo away, bird,"
she said, waving her arms at the birdhouse.
Both the bluebird and the sparrow scattered.

Acknowledgments

I am grateful to my parents and family for their encouragement, love, and patience. I know it has been hard.

Kevin and Judy O'Connor kindly let us borrow their cabin home in Asheville where bohemian culture and natural beauty inspired several key revisions.

I want to thank my friends and colleagues for their encouragement, especially Thomas Boguszewski, Matthew Byars, and Douglas Finkel—true artists. Likewise, Jim Moore was there for me when I needed a mentor in the difficult time after the workshops were done.

Partly, I wrote this book for my students over the years. The memory of our countless hours reading and laughing through so many classics together deserved an entirely different kind of Young Adult book. I wanted to invent a future so much better than the popular titles on the store shelves—dystopian science fiction, miserable memoirs, vampire romances—ever allowed them to expect.

This volume never would have seen another reader without John Lemon, my editor and publisher. He took a chance on *Clair* because he believes in the epic form. The expertise—and freedom—he lent in his tireless comments and correspondences were most welcome.

About the Author

Photo: Douglas Finkel

E.C. Hansen lives, runs, and writes in Maryland. His work has appeared in *North American Review, Water~Stone Review, The St. Paul Almanac, Reality Sandwich,* and other publications. *The Epic of Clair* is his first major work. You can follow him on Twitter @echansenpoet and at www.echansenpoet.com.

ILIUM
PRESS

If you enjoyed this book, the author and the publisher encourage you to post a favorable review with your favorite online bookseller. If you would like to be notified of upcoming releases from the Ilium Press, please visit our website at www.iliumpress.com, or visit and "like" the Ilium Press page on Facebook.

www.ingramcontent.com/pod-product-compliance
Lightning Source LLC
Chambersburg PA
CBHW020245150626
46552CB00020B/215